IN HELEN'S HANDS

by

Nanisi Barrett D'Arnuk

2020

IN HELEN'S HANDS

ISBN 13: 978-1-63555-639-1

This Trade Paperback Original Is Published By
Bold Strokes Books, Inc.
P.O. Box 249
Valley Falls, NY 12185

First Edition: January 2020

CREDITS
Editor: Barbara Ann Wright
Production Design: Stacia Seaman
Cover Design by Tammy Seidick

For Ti, with love

Chapter One

Most times a moment just passes me by, unnoticed, but when I look back, it's that one instant that changed my life forever. I could have said that it was when I first unwrapped a Christmas present and heard her magnificent music for the first time, or maybe it was when I saw her, standing there backstage, beside the nine-foot Baldwin grand. But I prefer to think of it as the one flash in my life when that beautiful ebony hand reached out, took the glass from the bartender, and handed me my drink. I'll remember that moment for as long as I live. It was as if I'd been seared with an electric probe, and it was instantly etched in my mind.

The after-concert party at the arts center was in full swing, and everyone was in a great mood. There'd been other parties, other concerts, but this was very special. Helen Robins, one of the best and hottest jazz pianists of the century, was making a national tour to sell her latest album, and she'd been getting rave reviews throughout the country. There was a rumor that she was also going to Asia and then back to Europe. Also, this one-night concert in Boston was supposed to be the last stop before she went home to New York to write the music for her next album.

I'd felt blessed to be among the fifteen-piece pit orchestra that had backed her final number in this concert, the world premiere of a twenty-minute jazz cantata with singers, Helen's finest work to date. The art center's professional singers, four men and three women, had been working on the music for weeks. I knew because I'd played piano for every rehearsal and Ann, my current lover, was one of the singers.

I'd have thought I'd be jaded because we did a guest artist concert three or four times a year. I could add some of the best names in the business to my resume. But this concert was Helen Robins. There was no comparison. My childhood piano teacher had given me one of her records while I was still in high school, and I remember playing it until the grooves were almost worn through. She'd been my idol since I began playing serious jazz piano several years before. I couldn't believe I'd actually played on the same program as her, even if I was only an unseen piano player in the pit. It was so exciting!

When I'd first seen her from the wings, Helen had seemed engrossed in a discussion with Jack, who directed the pit orchestra. She'd had on a dark red silk pantsuit that caught the light with shimmers of black and showed off her dark skin and trim figure. Her shoes had a very stylish low heel. Her makeup was absolutely stunning. Although she wasn't tall next to Jack, I could tell she was a couple inches taller than me. Every move she made was graceful and flowing like her music.

As I'd watched Helen, my mind couldn't help but imagine what it might be like to feel those hands on my skin, her lips against mine, the feel of those arms wrapping around me...

And there she'd been, no more than twenty feet away, going over music. I'd heard so much about her, about her music and her style, and I'd listened to her recordings so many times that I felt as if I already knew her. But the reality of seeing her standing there, leaning casually against the piano, was something I hadn't expected. It took my breath away. I'd felt a hand on my shoulder. It was the lead sax player.

"You ready, Mickey?" he'd asked.

"Always have to be."

"Good. See you out there." He'd walked away. I'd taken a deep breath and followed.

And the concert had been breathtaking. The cantata had gotten a standing ovation, and the audience hadn't let her off the stage until she'd played three encores. Now at the party, she was ensconced in the far corner of the room with my boss, Andrew, as he played host/devoted lackey as person after person paid homage, all those who'd paid the extra couple hundred dollars or more to get "sponsor tickets" so they could sit close during the concert, go to this party, and drop her name at their next dinner party.

She laughed and talked amicably, sharing asides with Andrew, sipping from a champagne glass, and waving a long brown cigarette.

The cigarettes were a trademark. I'd read somewhere that they were made especially for her in New York: Shermans, seven or eight inches long of natural tobacco, mild and filtered. In her hands, a shorter cigarette, even one hundred millimeters, would look dwarfed. She wielded it like a conductor's baton, the length only enhancing her graceful hands. I was mesmerized by the way she manipulated it.

I hung back, nursing my rum and ginger ale, observing her out of the corner of my eye. She'd changed from the long black gown she'd performed in and was now clad in that astonishing, form-fitting, red silk suit she'd worn before the concert. I had to concentrate to keep from staring. My heart seemed to be bumping out the rhythm to the cantata, and I didn't want to make a starstruck fool of myself in front of her.

I tried making small talk with the other musicians from the orchestra or staff from the center, but I was always aware of her and doing my best to appear above it all.

Stephen, the sax player, had already asked me to go home with him. We'd been flirting and teasing all night, our usual habit. He asked me every time we played in the same show, but I'd coquettishly deferred tonight. He was fun to flirt with, and the one time I had gone home with him after an all-night recording session, it had been wonderful fun sex, but I hadn't been able to sit comfortably for two days after.

Tonight, I wasn't in the mood for Stephen even though Ann had already disappeared to God-knew-where. I shrugged. Ann and I weren't communicating all that well, and she'd probably gone off with one of the guys or gals in the crew. I knew she'd been spending a lot of time backstage, flirting with the two new lighting technicians.

I was about to reach over the bar for my third rum and ginger when a long, graceful arm took my drink from the bartender and held it out to me.

"Andrew tells me you do transcriptions."

I slowly turned, my eyes glued to the graceful, dark-skinned hand holding my drink, my heart beating a quick gallop. I hoped my hand wasn't shaking so badly that I'd splash the syrupy blend all over the place.

"Thank you," I said as I took the drink. Then I looked up into Helen's clear, beautiful face. The dark eyes seemed to bore through me, capturing me in an invisible web.

"Yes. I transcribe and arrange some," I mumbled.

"Do you get to New York often?" she asked as she reached for a glass of champagne.

I could have melted into the warmth of her voice, and the light smell of her jasmine perfume started my head spinning. Was I starting to sweat? "I can."

"Good. I'm writing an opera, and I hate taking the time to write music when it's so much easier to record my thoughts and have someone else write them down. I do have to let the singers know what they're supposed to sing." She chuckled, a dark contralto breath, then sipped her drink and gave me a warm smile as her eyes traveled the length of my body. "I'll send you a tape. Call me." And with that, she turned and walked away.

I just stood there holding my drink for I'm not sure how long.

"Something else, isn't she?"

The voice startled me. I'd been so engrossed in watching Helen I hadn't heard Frank come up behind me.

I turned and smiled. "I'm not sure how to take all of this," I whispered, not sure there was anything else happening in the room.

"Just take what's offered and say thank you." He chuckled, a big smile across his face.

I shook my head. He knew me too well and had the nerve to call me on it. He knew my secret thoughts and was privy to all the indiscretions I'd had with both men and women while Ann was busy elsewhere. Too bad he was gay. He would have made an interesting lover.

"She asked for information on all the musicians in the orchestra tonight," Frank said. I nodded. Helen was known for taking a personal interest in everyone she shared a stage with. I'd read a quote she made: "Making music is like having sex: When it's good and the music climaxes, it's nice to know who you came with."

I laughed. "Who'd she ask?"

"Andrew."

"Shit." I frowned. Andrew was my boss, but more importantly, he was also Ann's protective cousin who didn't approve of our relationship. Not that he was anti-gay, far from it. He'd been known to make his own little forays on both sides of the track. He just didn't like me playing around in his family. There was respect between us but also a certain distance. I'd never have used him as a reference.

"Well? What did she say to you? Does she want your body or your mind? Are you going home with her? Does Ann know?"

I turned to him as I took a long gulp of my drink.

"I think she may have just offered me a job."

"I know she grilled Andrew about you," Frank whispered.

"How do you always hear these things?"

"I am the proverbial fly on the wall, my dear." He smiled smugly. "And I have twenty-twenty hearing."

"Then what else did you hear?"

"She liked the way Stephen plays sax. She may write something for him to play on her next album. And"—he hesitated—"she wanted to know what your commitments are."

I scowled. "And Andrew said I have none."

"He said he could spare you for a few weeks and that you were completely free."

I wondered if that was wishful thinking on Andrew's part or if he knew something I didn't. Ann and I would have to talk one of these days, the sooner the better.

Maybe New York was what I needed. Besides, a few days away from Boston seemed like a nice diversion. It was early April, and my teaching schedule for the summer was still up in the air. A few extra days in the Big Apple could give me the perspective I needed to get back to work. I'd neglected my own composing and playing in the past few months, letting Ann and my work at the center push everything else aside. Maybe I needed this step back to get my creative juices flowing again.

"Helen did seem more than interested," Frank added. "She lowered her voice so I couldn't hear, but I think she asked some very personal questions. Andrew seemed more than willing to give her answers."

I glanced over to where Helen was next to Andrew, graciously accepting all the lavish praises heaped on her by people who'd paid big money. Before I could glance away, Andrew's eyes met mine. A look of curious amusement crossed his face before he returned his attention to Helen.

I decided it was time to go home whether I could find Ann or not.

❖

Sunday afternoon after the concert, Andrew dropped by the apartment to pick Ann up for a family gathering and had brought a large manila envelope for me. I opened it and looked inside, but when I saw the monogram across the letterhead, I stopped and just held the envelope until Andrew and Ann had driven off.

Inside was a brief note and a small reel of quarter-track tape. The letter, on heavy gray parchment with a flowing "H.R." in the upper right-hand corner, was short and to the point.

"Transcribe this. We can talk about it in New York in a few weeks. Call me when it's finished." Her address and phone number were embossed across the bottom.

I looked at the tape in my hand, realizing for the first time what I held. This was music that no one else had heard before, music that Helen Robins had created and played. I was about to become one of the first, if not *the* first, person to hear Helen Robin's work-in-progress. My hands shook as I threaded the tape through my tape deck and slipped the headphones over my ears. Sitting back, I pushed the "play" button. After a few seconds of white noise, the sound of her piano began.

I couldn't believe my ears. Her style was clear, but the passion and power of the music made the simplicity of the lilting melody seem like a feather floating amidst the rages of a thunderstorm. The work was gorgeous; her left-hand work breathtaking. Definitely her best work thus far.

As I pushed the rewind button, it hit me…I was supposed to listen to this and then write it down, note for note, just as she'd played it. I closed my eyes. Yes, I'd transcribed music from tape before; choral or popular stuff mostly, even some of Andrew's arrangements for the singers. And I'd orchestrated some of his work for the stage band, but this task was above and beyond anything I had ever conceived of doing. Would it have been easier if it had been a full orchestra? Then I could have listened, picked out separate instruments, and written each down separately. But this was just one pianist. Just. One. Pianist. One pianist with twenty-four fingers on each of her seventeen hands.

I let my head fall forward into my hands.

Was this something I could do? Was it something anyone could do? Damn, I so much wanted to impress her. I imagined those eyes smiling at me, telling me what a good job I'd done, how proud she was of me.

Well, that was shot to shit.

I turned off the tape deck and went out in search of some food and a good stiff drink.

❖

I woke up and looked at the clock: 4:00 a.m. I got out of bed and headed for the bathroom. The fried chicken I'd gotten for dinner at a cute little restaurant still lay heavy in my stomach, and the taste of beer and cigarettes I'd had at the bar across the street from it had turned into a sour paste in my mouth.

I made the mistake of looking in the mirror as I rinsed my

hands and put the toothbrush back in its holder. The face there looked back at me accusingly. *You're chicken-shit*, it seemed to be saying. *You gave up without even trying.*

I stared back.

Yes, I have. I hadn't even listened a second time. How did I know I couldn't do the transcription? Was this my big break? Would working with Helen Robins open new doors for me? Even just studying her music could help me. And above all that, I could get to know the woman I'd been admiring.

I balanced the opportunities against the risks.

Oh, what the hell, I thought, what did I have to lose? *I might even learn something.*

❖

The two weeks after the concert were very strange. Without really talking about why or what was happening, Ann left the bedroom we'd shared on the second floor of our apartment in the South End and turned the den into her bedroom. We were still talking as friends, but we both made it a point not to mention anything personal, and Ann was staying away from home many more evenings than she usually did. I heard her come in very late several times without dropping by my room to say good night. Many times, she didn't come home until I was getting ready for work the next morning. I knew she was dating someone else, but I never asked who. I didn't want to know.

I guess I was too busy to actually think about it. Once I'd made the decision to try the transcriptions, I poured every waking moment into it. I'd listen to a few measures, write what I thought I heard, play it on the piano, listen again, and make corrections, then listen to some more. Many times, I had to listen again and again to make sure I had it correctly. I walked around in a daze, feeling as if my ears were bleeding. I became obsessed with the project and even raced home between classes and rehearsals to work some more. I missed meals and was functioning on about four hours of sleep.

I hoped it would be worth it. The one thing that kept me going was that thought of Helen smiling at me. So I kept at it and finally had the five-minute segment from the tape down on paper.

I couldn't put it off any more, so with a prayer and my fingers crossed, I dialed the number on the stationary.

A young voice answered the phone. I introduced myself and asked to speak to Helen. I could hear the sound of a hand covering the phone and the mumble of voices. Before I could take a breath, Helen's beautiful voice was on the other end. My heart stopped. I was actually talking to Helen Robins, *the* Helen Robins, on my very own phone.

"Have you finished it?" she asked.

"I think so," I said. "There's one spot I can't get, but I think the rest is done."

"Good." I could hear the smile in her voice. "Bring it down a week from Monday, and I'll check through it. I have a lot more for you to work on. I'll put a check in the mail for you today. We can negotiate everything else when you get here."

I gave her my address, and she hung up.

I stood there like a fool, staring at the phone in my hand. I was going to visit Helen Robins in her home in ten days, and she was paying me to visit. My hands started to shake.

Chapter Two

The train ride from Boston to New York City seemed to take forever. Maybe it was my nervousness, but I felt as if I'd never get there even though it took only three hours.

I'd decided to spend some of the money Helen sent and checked into a sleazy little hotel just off Washington Square in the Village rather than stay with friends. I knew Rhonda would have been more than happy to let me stay in her fifth-floor walk-up in midtown, but Rhonda was Ann's friend, not mine. It'd be easier not to have to talk about what was or wasn't happening between Ann and me. Rhonda probably knew more about it than I did.

Besides, the last time we'd stayed with Rhonda, she'd asked Ann and me to help carry some grocery bags back to the apartment. The four-block walk and the fifth-floor climb hadn't been a problem, but when we started unloading the bags, we found marijuana and cocaine at the bottom of each bag. It hit us then how Rhonda was paying for her beautiful clothes and high living style. I didn't want to be involved in that again, especially this time.

I registered, then went out in search of the subway. It stopped at every station for over eighty blocks. Then it took what seemed like hours to walk from the subway to Helen's address. I knew that the Upper West Side was a busy place, but it seemed to have that knack of holding my target at bay. The streets knew I longed to get to Helen's as soon as possible, so they continued to put both vehicular and foot traffic in front of me.

Finally, for a moment, I stood looking up at the massive old stone building that covered half the block. It was one of the older buildings not far from the river, built during the earlier part of the twentieth century. It wasn't right on the river, but I could tell that the apartments on the top floors had wonderful views. I hadn't expected opulence, but why not? A celebrity lived here.

I clutched the envelope with my work and prayed that Helen would approve of it and I wouldn't make a fool of myself when I opened my mouth.

The doorman called up to Helen's apartment, then directed me to the elevators.

"Fourth floor. Turn right," were his only words.

I took the elevator, listening to the old mechanisms grind, and walked down the corridor to my right. I took a deep breath and pushed the button next to the door marked "4D."

The door was opened by a slim young woman dressed in a T-shirt and the shortest shorts I'd ever seen. She had short mousey-brown hair and a low-cut top beneath a very pretty face.

"Hi, I'm—"

She cut me off. "Yeah, I know. Come on in."

At first, I was surprised by her curtness, but as I entered the apartment, my attention was taken by the massiveness of it. This was one of those old New York apartments that I only read about or saw on the 1950s and '60s TV shows. It was a relic that had escaped the "divide and get more money" mentality that had taken apartments like this and made them into smaller one- and two-bedroom units that would bring in more revenue for the owner and add more residents to the neighborhood.

I walked through the entry hall, which opened into a very formal living room. It was dominated by a long white leather couch surrounded by a cluster of leather chairs: two red, with heavy mahogany arms and legs, the third, an overstuffed wingback of black leather. The tables that dotted the room were all of matching mahogany. On the floor lay a beautiful Persian rug, mostly black and white with dots of red and gold threaded through it.

Beyond the massive sofas and chairs, I could see a baby grand through open doors into the next room. On the left was an immense staircase, carpeted in black and white, which wound up past the massively high ceiling.

"What did you bring?" Helen asked, omitting any greeting as she entered from a room to the right. She was dressed in a long, navy-blue silk dressing gown with blue mules on her feet. Her hair and makeup were perfect. The color of the gown against her dark skin gave her a very ethereal look.

"Just this." I smiled, trying to keep the awe out of my voice as I held out the manila envelope.

"Great. Would you like some iced tea or coffee?"

"Coffee would be nice," I said, hoping that there'd be some conversation between us.

"Neisy." She nodded toward the slender girl, who disappeared into the next room.

"Let me look at this," Helen said, taking my manuscript out of the package as she sank into the big black chair. "Have a seat."

Without taking her eyes off the first sheet of music, she reached into the large oak humidor on the table beside her chair and withdrew one of her infamous cigarettes.

I lowered myself onto the sofa, a little uneasy as Helen began to scan the music. I was nervous, like a child watching a teacher grade a paper. I took the cup of coffee that Neisy handed me and declined cream and sugar but kept my eyes on Helen's face. Neisy held out a lighter to Helen's cigarette, then disappeared again into the next room. I figured it must be a kitchen or pantry.

I watched her leave, puzzled. She was responding to Helen like an employee, maybe a maid, but her dress, or lack thereof, astounded me. Her shorts, which almost rode up into her crack, showed almost everything she had. I could see she wasn't wearing underwear. I also noticed a long red mark across the bottom of one butt cheek, like a welt or scar, or as if she'd sat on the edge of a hard bench for a long while. I turned my attention back to Helen as I sipped my coffee.

It was hard to discern what she was thinking. At moments, there'd be a smile, then a frown, then intense studying. I sipped the coffee anxiously. After what seemed like hours, she laid the music down and looked up at me.

"Not bad," she said matter-of-factly. "There are some problems, but you got most of it. I may change some of it now that I see it on paper, but all in all..." She shrugged and let the sentence hang as she crushed her cigarette in an antique ashtray. She rose. "Be here at nine tomorrow morning, and we'll go over this."

I stared. Was that a compliment or a condemnation?

I thought she was merely going to walk away, but she stopped. "Don't be such a frightened rabbit." She smirked. "You look like you've been caught in the headlights." She reached out and patted my cheek, then continued up the stairs and disappeared.

I watched her go, still feeling her hand on my face. Was that it? Had I traveled all this way to merely be told to come back tomorrow? I felt like the Cowardly Lion waiting for his chance to see the Great Wizard of Oz.

I turned to Neisy, who stood at the doorway. She'd watched Helen walk up the stairs, then turned to me.

"Is that it?" I asked. "Is she always so…abrupt?" I set my coffee on the table.

Neisy spoke for the first time since I'd entered the room. "Actually, that's the happiest I've seen her in over a month." She walked past me as if expecting me to follow and opened the door to let me out.

"I guess I'll see you tomorrow," I said as I left.

"I guess." She shrugged as she closed the door behind me.

Abruptness seemed to be the modus operandi here.

❖

As I took the subway back downtown, questions flooded my mind. One of the first was Neisy. Who was she? I'd never seen a maid in shorts that short before, but then, how many maids had I ever seen?

I got off at West Fourth Street and walked up the street. I was in Greenwich Village. Everything shook with energy. Everyone hurried to get someplace to sit and relax, then they quickly walked away. It was a pace I hadn't experienced in Boston.

That night, I changed into a fresh shirt and went out into the Village. I'd never been there alone before, but the thought of exploring this haven of LGBT lifestyle excited me.

I promised myself the run of the city. I'd worked hard for the past few weeks, and from the sound of Helen's comments, I might not have free time for another few weeks. I'd check out several of the bars around Sheridan Square but first, my rumbling stomach reminded me that I should stop into

Tiffany's or another coffee shop for a quick sandwich. On the way toward Seventh Avenue, I passed the window of the Pink PussyCat. Almost embarrassed to have someone see me gawking at the sex toys hanging in the window, I nevertheless stopped and gawked at the sex toys hanging in the window. Something about them, the mystery, the danger, something, caused my stomach to churn. I felt an excited heat in my crotch. I'd read about these but never seen them before. My college dorm-mates had giggled about some of them. Did people really use these?

I hurried past the store.

❖

I was at Helen's door at precisely 9:00 a.m. the next morning. I'd walked around the block twice to eat up the time because I'd gotten there twenty minutes early. The doorman waved me to the elevators as he called upstairs to announce me.

Neisy opened the door before I'd rung the bell. Still brusque, she pointed into the next room where Helen was busy at the piano, then disappeared into a room to the right.

I marched into the piano room and smiled. "Good morning."

"Ah, good, you're here." She stood up. "Play this for me."

She stepped aside as I slid onto the piano bench and looked at the all-too-familiar manuscript. I played the section she indicated. When I finished, Helen shook her head and laughed.

"Classical training, huh?"

"Yes, I have my master's from New England Conservatory."

"It's a shame." She smiled. "Classical training has ruined

some of the best jazz musicians. Here, play a C7 in the lower octave." As I started to reach for the chord, she pressed my hand onto the keyboard. "Don't be so careful. Straighten your fingers. No nice curves." She took my hand and adjusted it. "Just throw and hit. Don't cover and press."

I looked up. It was a direct conflict with everything I'd studied in the past ten years.

Helen smiled. "If you want to play good jazz, it has to start here." She tapped my chest. "Don't even worry about how your fingers look. They'll follow your heart. I promise." When I nodded, she said, "Now, let's go over some of these runs. I'm almost afraid that they can't be notated. But you made a good attempt."

We sat at the piano for the rest of the morning, going over her chordal voicings. Her hands were delicate but just enough larger than mine that I hadn't gotten every chord exact. I knew what I heard, but there were times when her fingers hit more than one note at a time. Those were the places that had me confused. Once I began to understand her style, it seemed to fall into place.

At lunchtime, we took a break. Neisy had sandwiches ready, beautiful smoked turkey with crisp lettuce and slices of tomatoes. When she placed the tray on the table, she looked at me.

"What do you drink with your meals?" she asked.

"Whatever you have."

"The only thing we always have is this blasted carrot and celery juice that Miss Robins insists on." The way she exaggerated Helen's name almost sounded disrespectful.

"It's good for you," Helen said.

"It's good for *you*," Neisy parried. Then she turned to me again. "There's some Coke or ginger ale if you prefer. I sneak it in when she isn't looking."

"Coke would be great." With that, Neisy turned and disappeared into the kitchen.

"Brat!" Helen called after her. "8:06 tomorrow night!"

I didn't know what was happening, but I didn't want to be stuck in the middle. I concentrated on my sandwich and downed the glass of Coke Neisy had set in front of me.

CHAPTER THREE

Tuesday had been a day of work, work, and more work. We went over all of the pages I had brought, and Helen gave me another stack of tapes to transcribe. I was going to be very busy.

When I finally left Helen's apartment at 6:30, I could barely drag myself back to my hotel. Once back at the hotel, I fell into bed without even thinking about eating. I was too tired to think, and the melodies and jazz riffs I'd been transcribing still ran through my brain whether I wanted them to or not.

Wednesday was no different. I listened and transcribed and listened some more. I was totally engulfed in the music. Nothing else could fit into my brain. I had finished for the day and waited at the copy service on the corner for them to duplicate the music. I was about to hail a cab to take me to a women's bar in the East Village when I realized I still held the music. I would have no place to put it, and I didn't want to lose it, so I turned back to Helen's.

The doorman waved to me as I headed for the elevators and made my way to Helen's door. She'd given me a key so I could go in and work when she wasn't home. I trotted through the living room and set the music on the piano.

I could hear crying coming from upstairs. It sounded like

Neisy, much too young to be Helen, and she seemed to be in a lot of pain.

I hastened up the stairs to see if I could help and went toward a door that was ajar. Quietly, I opened it and looked inside.

It was a dimly lit room with strange shadows making the bizarre interior scary. Strips of leather and chains hung from the ceiling. Odd-looking pieces of furniture were scattered around the room, but my eyes were riveted to the far wall.

Neisy was naked, hanging limply by her wrists from chains that hung well above her head. Ugly red welts lined her back and butt. I could see her sobs as they shook her body. A small spotlight illuminated her. Behind her, holding a short black whip, stood Helen.

I watched as twice more, Helen made fresh red stripes across Neisy's back.

"Please, Mistress," Neisy cried. "Please. Enough. I beg you."

Helen just laughed and let another swing of the whip fall very close to the bottom of Neisy's ass.

Neisy let out a wail and tried to press farther into the wall.

Realization of what I was witnessing slowly crept into my mind. I'd heard about this type of sex-play but had never seen it, never knew anyone who practiced it.

I didn't realize Helen even knew I was there until she was standing in front of me. I couldn't read the look on her face. Amusement? Anger?

"Well?" she said.

My breath was coming out in short quick gasps. I glanced past Helen, barely able to take my eyes off of Neisy's back.

"I...I'm sorry..." I managed. "I heard her crying..."

Helen looked at me with a very evil-looking grin. "Would you like to join us?"

I looked into her eyes, now aware that she was enjoying my discomfort. Oh my God! What should I do? Should I just leave?

Without waiting, she said, "Take your clothes off. The only person allowed to be clothed in this room is me."

I stood there like a zombie, my eyes still on Neisy as Helen unbuttoned my shirt and let it fall over my shoulders. I didn't usually wear a bra, so as it fell away, it brushed my nipples. I looked down at them. They were standing out like flagpoles. Was I that turned on? Then she unzipped my shorts, which fell to the floor, and I realized how wet my panties felt. I wasn't even sure what was happening, I was dumbstruck as I glanced back at Neisy.

Helen walked back over to Neisy and whispered something in her ear as she caressed her head and shoulders. Neisy nodded, and Helen turned her attention back to me. "This is new to you," Helen said.

I guess I nodded because she gave a quick laugh and stepped back to me, even closer than before. As she crossed behind me, I felt her hot breath on my ear.

"But it excites you?" She reached into my bikinis and ran her finger slowly across my cunt hair. "Oh yes, it does excite you, doesn't it?" She chuckled as she felt the wetness between my legs. I tried to swallow, to put some moisture back in my mouth as her fingers probed me. The feel of her touch sent shock waves throughout my body. Was Helen Robins really touching me? Was this what I had dreamed about for years?

"And you don't know what to do about it." It seemed to amuse her. She closed the door. and slowly walked around me. "Kneel down and observe."

I don't remember agreeing, but there I was, on my knees.

She returned to Neisy and cranked the wheel on the wall to lower the chains. Neisy sank slowly against her. As she released Neisy's wrists, Helen held her lovingly and rocked her back and forth. Neisy seemed to relax into her as the tears still streamed down her face. Finally, Helen's voice broke the silence. "Well, Neisy, this bad little girl seems to have interrupted us. Do you think she needs to be punished for barging in here uninvited?"

Neisy seemed to recognize me for the first time. She nodded slowly. "Yes, Mistress," she whispered, her breath still ragged as her tears subsided. "She interrupted uninvited."

"And you weren't completely finished, were you?" Helen asked.

"No. Mistress, I wasn't finished." An evil look crossed her face as she stared at me.

I began to get frightened that this would disappear; that it was all a dream. "I…I just came up because I heard her crying…"

"Quiet!"

I jumped as Helen's voice boomed out.

"There are rules in this room. Either obey them or leave right now. Rule one, don't speak unless you've been given permission." Helen helped Neisy to the floor, then strolled up to me. "Do you want to stay, or do you want to leave?"

I knelt there with my mouth open. Did I want to go?

Helen pulled a stool up and sat. "If you stay, you will relinquish all rights within this room. You will be here solely for my pleasure, not your own, and you will obey everything I say. No matter what. Do you understand?"

I didn't. Not fully.

Helen leaned closer as she reached out and caressed my cheek. "Confused?"

I nodded, my mouth still open.

"Then we will start slowly. This is my room. You will not come in here again without my permission. Once you cross that threshold, you will obey everything I say, and you will not question it. Is that understood?" I nodded. "If you disobey, you will be severely punished, but if you please me, you will be rewarded." She glanced at Neisy, who was wiping her face with a towel. "Neisy is my slave, my sweet little girl. She has earned that status by pleasing me. You will be subservient to her as well as to me until you prove your worth. What happens in this room stays in this room."

She studied me.

"If you have questions, ask. There are very strict rules here; don't guess at the answers." She released the clasp that held my shoulder-length hair back and ran her fingers through. Grabbing a handful, she pushed my head back. Tears came to my eyes as the pain seared my scalp.

"Neisy," she commanded, "bring the paddle."

It felt strange that I didn't mind the pain, and it aroused me even more. It almost felt right. Was that wrong?

Helen let go of my hair as Neisy handed her the black paddle. As she laid out the rules, I watched her turn the short leather paddle over and over in her hands. "You will feel pain because it pleases me to give you pain. And you will be grateful that I have allowed you to please me. You will not complain or refuse to obey me. Is that clear?"

I looked at her as I slowly nodded.

"You'll begin to welcome the pain. It will become a sign of my love for you." She stopped as she again grabbed my hair. Her voice was lower, softer when she spoke again. "You'll want to be able to take as much as I want to give you, but there will be times when you'll be unable to satisfy me. If you've tried, tried very hard, but find you can't go on, you'll have a special word. If…when…you use it, I'll stop. It'll be your safeguard, your safety word. Use it carefully. Using it too often will greatly displease me. Do you understand?"

I nodded, some of the terror beginning to ebb. At least I had a way out if I got in over my head. I wanted to laugh. Over my head? Damn, I was already in way over my head. What had I gotten into? My stomach started to flip with nervous anticipation. Was this the way I really wanted to please Helen Robins?

Helen chuckled. "We'll start slowly, little one." She leered. "But I have every confidence that you will not disappoint me. Will you?"

I looked into her eyes. No, I didn't want to disappoint her. If this was what pleased her, what made her happy, then I was in it. I wanted to show her how strong and tough I was, how I could give her everything she asked for. I was sure my eyes were still wide.

Without waiting, she pulled my hair, and I sprawled across her lap like a child awaiting a spanking. "Is Boston your home?" she asked.

"Yes."

"That will be your safe word. If you cannot continue, just say Boston, and I will stop. But use it judiciously. Using it too often is likely to make me very angry." She forced my panties down over my ass. I took a deep breath as her hand brushed there, slightly filling me with trepidation.

"Neisy," she said, "it was you she interrupted. You'll take the first swing."

I started to object but Helen's firm grasp on the back of my neck prevented me from moving. I jumped as the first whack of the leather paddle hit my rear. The pain spread through me, harder than I'd imagined it would be.

"Again." A second, then a third, then a fourth landed. My breath was ragged, tears already wanting to escape my eyes.

"Now, these are from me," Helen whispered. "Don't disappoint me."

Before I could draw my next breath, I was struck with a whack far fiercer than the first ones had been. I moaned as the pain spread through my entire body. I gripped the chair leg beneath me and held it as tightly as I could. As the shock of the paddle began to subside, I felt another pain, harder and more intense than anything I'd ever thought could be. As whack after whack hit me, I wasn't even sure where I was being hit; my entire being seemed completely engulfed in the pain. I wasn't even sure I was still conscious, but my heart was singing. The pain added a thrill.

At last, I realized that the beating had stopped. How long ago, I wasn't even sure. I began to realize that I no longer gripped the chair leg but held desperately to two hands. I tried to draw a breath, but it was ragged, hesitant, as any movement brought the pain back again. I stared into Neisy's eyes as she knelt in front of me, holding my clenched hands.

"Very good, little one," Helen cooed close to my ear. "For a first try, you have pleased me."

I still gasped in short, quick breaths. Tears and sweat covered my face. Helen caressed my neck with one hand as she gently wiped my face with a soft towel.

"Well, Neisy!" Helen laughed. "I think we have ourselves a new houseboy. What do you think? Should we keep it? Or throw it back in the street?"

There was a moment of silence.

"We could keep it for a while, Mistress, as long as it amuses us."

Helen laughed again as she caressed my back. "You have earned a reward tonight. You did well, for your first time." The words seemed like music. "Neisy, help this new little houseboy to the horse."

"Yes, Mistress," Neisy said as she lifted me from Helen's lap.

As she laid me over an upholstered bench, she whispered in my ear. "Such a good little girl to please the mistress so much on your first try. We like to please the mistress, don't we? Keep at it and you stay."

I slumped forward over the bench which was just a few inches short of waist-high. I felt so weak, so drained, I couldn't have held myself up if I'd tried. I saw a series of handles along the other side. Neisy placed my hands on one set.

"Hang on tight," she whispered and stepped back.

Helen's hands on my ass felt cool and soft as she gently stroked my aching flesh. I closed my eyes, letting the cold of her hands soothe some of the fire that still raged in my skin.

Soon, Helen's hands worked their way closer to my cunt, and her fingers gently caressed my lips, softly probing, gently pushing into me. First one finger, then two, then three.

"Oh, yes, oh, yes," I moaned. I loved the feel of her touching me.

But Helen just chuckled. "You think so, eh?" She laughed and added her fourth finger and her thumb and drove her whole hand deep within me.

I held my breath. That hand, that beautiful hand that had seemed so small and graceful yesterday was suddenly the largest, most merciless weapon in the world. I was lost between ecstasy and devastation. I could feel her flexing her fingers, feel her fist pulsing larger and larger, felt it twisting and turning within me. I'd lost hold of anything else. The only reality in existence was the pulsing hand within me. I knew I was going to die; I'd made my peace with the world, and I'd said good-bye to anything else. Everything except that magnificent fist balled up in my heart and brain and the sublime pain as it pushed into me and pulled back again. And in the midst of the pain, I was coming. I could feel my muscles starting to tense.

Her other hand dug deeply into the bruises on my ass cheeks. I let out a weak moan. "Hold on to it, my little girl." She was laughing. "I'll let you know when you can come. You'll wait until I give you permission. I haven't finished fucking you yet."

Then she rammed her fist even harder. As she continued, I started to plunge over the edge. Only Neisy's grip on my arms, her nails digging into me, gave me the strength to continue. My safety word roared through my brain as Helen encompassed my being.

Only her words kept me from yelling "Boston." "Oh, yes, little girl. You are so hot. And so tight! This is very good. Give me all you can."

My body felt as if it was going to explode. My brain was on the verge of spilling out my ears. I didn't think I could go on. I didn't think…I didn't think. I just felt. And felt.

Then I heard the most wonderful words I'd ever heard. "Yes! Come to me. Now!"

I let go of anything tangible as my body erupted. I let it happen. I gave up whatever thread of control I thought I had. I didn't want it. I just wanted to be awash in the feelings that surrounded me. The orgasms—there had to have been many more than one—washed over me, drowning me in sensations. Would it ever stop?

Finally, as my body started to relax, Helen pulled her hand from me. Again I came, hard.

Slowly, I became aware of Neisy prying my hands from the handles, which I'd held in a death grip. I slumped against the horse. Where had they taken my legs? I knew I had them when I came in here.

Helen pulled me back, and I sagged to the floor, finally realizing that I lay in her arms, my head against her shoulder. Her arms were around me as I lay covered with sweat and tears. It took several minutes to realize where I was and what had just happened.

She held me tightly, rocking me. As my breathing started to slow, she stroked my hair.

"You will be such a wonderful little girl. There is so much to teach you, and you learn so quickly." She continued rocking me as I sank into her. I started to become aware of my surroundings as my breath started to even out. I looked up into Neisy's face. The smile she gave me made me feel almost as warm as Helen's arms did.

Helen laid me on the soft carpet and started to get up. "Just rest a while," she whispered. "I have other business to finish."

As she caressed my face, I felt myself drifting off to sleep.

Chapter Four

I was still on the floor beside the horse when I awoke Thursday morning. Someone had wrapped a blanket over me. I was cozy and warm. The lights in the room were slightly brighter. Dressed in a white cotton robe that was so sheer I could see the red streaks across her ass, Neisy was cleaning up the remnants of last night. I watched her for a few moments as she lovingly washed each lash of the whip. I could hear her humming.

I moaned as every muscle in my body objected to my attempts to sit up.

"Well, well, good morning." Neisy smiled.

I smiled back weakly as I forced my aching body into a sitting position. My ass definitely did not want to be sat on today. And I had thought I was sore after my night with Stephen.

Neisy laughed and slid over to hand me a glass that had been on the floor next to her. "Drink this. You lost a lot of fluids last night."

I took a sip of the pink liquid. Peach juice! I could feel the cold liquid worming its way through my body to my stomach.

"Drink it all," Neisy ordered as she sank onto the floor in front of me. I drained the glass.

"What time is it?"

Neisy glanced over her shoulder at a large clock I hadn't

noticed before. "7:10 a.m. How do you feel?" she asked as she took the empty glass.

"I'm not sure. Am I still in one piece?"

Neisy laughed. It seemed out of character. I'd barely even seen her smile before. "Yes. One piece. And a great piece at that."

I joined her laughter. It felt good to be talking to her. It felt like a shared camaraderie.

"You did pretty good last night," she said. "I thought you were going to break a couple times, but you hung right in there. I was impressed. I know that one's first time can be rather terrifying."

I smiled. It felt good to be praised. I wondered how I'd survived last night. It was so different from what I'd imagined this sex life to be. I never thought I'd want some of the feelings I'd experienced just a few hours ago. "Can I ask a question?"

"Ask away. Helen said you'd probably be full of them this morning."

How could I phrase this? "Is it always so...well, is it always like this?"

Neisy smiled, almost to herself as she nodded. "Isn't she incredible? I adore her. I've been with a lot of dominants. Men and women. She's the first woman I've ever really admired. She's so strong. And sure. I love submitting to her." I could hear the love in her voice. "No, it's not always. Lately she's been preoccupied with something, but you seem to have lit a spark in her."

"Me?" I was amazed.

"Yes, you. Ever since she returned from Boston, it's been different. I didn't like you at first. I thought you were too weak...too vanilla...really wimpy, but Helen said you had potential. She just didn't know how to tap it. I guess your mistake last night was just plain dumb luck."

"Helen discussed me?"

Neisy looked at me, seemingly amused. "Yes, Helen discussed you. That surprises you?"

I stopped for a moment. "Well, yes."

"You really are just a baby, aren't you? You have no clue what you've gotten into." She sat back and studied me.

I shook my head.

"Well, my dear, I'll help with what I can. I'm probably crazy because I have the feeling that when you really start to learn the ropes, so to speak"—she chuckled at her own joke—"you'll probably replace me, and I'll be out on my ear." She seemed to think about it a moment. "Ironic, isn't it? I guess that's the mark of a good bottom, always think of your top's happiness first."

She got to her feet and held her hand out. "Come on, there's a lot to do today. I've got to show you how to care for all this stuff." She glanced around the room. "From now on, it's your job to clean up."

I took her hand and let her pull me to my feet.

She showed me around the room, explaining each piece of furniture and its use. There was the stool where Helen always sat, its padded seat oiled to swivel silently as she wished; the padded horse with handles; and the wide bench with metal eye bolts where ropes and chains could be attached. Neisy explained the chains hanging from their pulleys on the ceiling over the four-foot-wide platform built in the corner. And, of course, there was the armoire. As Neisy opened the large oak doors, I gawked at the wonder of a large assortment of whips, lashes, chains, shackles, belts, and many other forms of torture devices. Each had its own special place, carefully labeled, so that each was ready when needed.

"You'll learn what each is for." Neisy smiled at my wonder. "And you'll learn how to care for every one. The leather has to be carefully taken care of, especially if there's any blood on it. You have to make sure it's cleaned and sanitary and treated so it doesn't dry out. Dried leather hurts like a bitch."

She reached to the bottom shelf and took out the longest, thickes, dildo I'd ever seen. And I'd thought Stephen was big. This was much bigger and harder and attached to a thick black belt.

"This is my favorite." Neisy smiled, fondling the shaft. "Helen is a master at its use." She turned to me. "Have you fucked with a man?"

I nodded. "Yes, but no one quite that big."

Neisy chuckled as she put it back in its place on the shelf. "You'll never get enough. It's marvelous. Makes most men pale by comparison."

As she closed the doors of the armoire, a voice rang out behind us. "How's he doing?"

We looked up to see Helen standing in the doorway. I almost expected her to have transformed into an angel or a sinister apparition out of a Walt Disney movie, but there she stood in her jeans and soft, flowing shirt, the same Helen Robins who had greeted me on each previous morning.

"He'll be fine," Neisy answered.

I looked at her. I knew that I was now the "houseboy," but I still wasn't used to being referred by the masculine pronoun. Well, maybe I'd have to get used to it sooner or later.

"Any second thoughts?" Helen asked.

"I...don't know. I don't think so," I answered tentatively. I still wasn't sure what I'd gotten into except what I'd experienced last night.

Helen nodded thoughtfully. "Shower, dress, and come downstairs. We'll talk." With that, she turned and left.

I looked at Neisy, who shrugged and pointed toward

another door that was slightly ajar, a bathroom. "Don't keep her waiting. I'll finish up here. We can continue later."

Once again, I'd been dismissed and left with questions still rolling around in my head. Was this what I wanted, and what exactly was I getting into?

❖

When I went downstairs, Helen was in the music room at her desk, the same as she'd been that first Tuesday morning. Was that only two days ago? She was reviewing some of the manuscript I'd worked on yesterday. As I entered, she laid her pencil down and turned to me. Pointing to the floor in front of her, she said, "Have a seat."

I sat down, cross-legged, and waited. She studied me for a moment.

"Regrets about last night?" she asked.

I shook my head. "No." I didn't regret what had happened, but I wasn't sure where it was headed.

Helen smiled broadly. "I thought you'd enjoy it."

"Enjoy is a strange word. I don't think it would have been my first choice to describe it."

Helen laughed. "Do you want to change your mind? You can back out now if you want."

I stopped. How could I describe my feelings? I wanted to be with her, I wanted to be close, to be intimate, to make her happy. "I just hadn't considered this possibility before."

"And now?"

I thought for a moment. "I guess I'd have to know more about what I'm getting into."

"Have you any experience at all with sadomasochism or dominance and submission?"

I shook my head.

"None? Not even any movies? Fantasies? Anything?"

There was this one movie I'd gone to with Frank in Boston's Combat Zone, and the long discussion we'd had after, over a full bottle of rum, both of us admitting after a few glasses of the mellow blended malt how turned on we'd been.

"Well, maybe. Once. A movie. A while ago…and I read a couple books."

Helen laughed. "Don't consider those trash books real. They're nothing like this life. They're written for men to give themselves something to jack off to."

I nodded. It hadn't seemed real when I read it, but then, what did I know?

Helen looked at me thoughtfully. "Then let us negotiate a contract so you'll know your role and responsibilities. If you remain as my boy, it will have to be by your own informed consent. I don't want to be accused of raping, coercing, or intimidating you. You have to know what you're getting into. This is not a game to me. It is a lifestyle. There are others in this life, but we are hidden more than the average homosexual. Since the Stonewall riots, it has almost become acceptable to be queer, but it is still frowned upon to be sadomasochistic, especially since these wonderful feminists have raised their voices in the gay cause. It's all right to be queer as long as you do it their way. So we still stay hidden. You must know that what we do in that room upstairs cannot be told to anyone. If this was twenty or thirty years ago, not only could I be arrested, but you could be thrown into a mental institution."

"But even if we're only doing what we want?" I was still naive enough to ask.

"Things have changed. Soon we may be able to live it openly but not quite yet." She shook her head. "There are a lot of us but not enough. We can be open in certain areas but not everywhere. Maybe someday…"

We continued for a few minutes, discussing whether this type of life would ever truly be accepted. Then she changed the subject back to me.

"When I first saw you in Boston, you looked very feminine. I had to ask if you were straight or lesbian. Andrew said he thought you were bisexual. Are you?"

"I guess so. I never really analyzed it."

"In your lesbian relationships, are you a butch or a femme?"

I'd never considered that either. I knew I wasn't the masculine stereotypical dyke that I'd seen in some of the bars, but then, I wasn't the ultra-femme that always wore lipstick and eye shadow, either. I'd always taken control of the relationships. Always been the one to make decisions, do the manual work. Did that make me the butch?

"I guess I'm probably a bit…just a little butch," I decided.

Helen laughed. "Just a little butch? I like that. Just a little butch. Good. Then that's what you shall be. Little Butch. That will be my name for you. Yes, I do like that. Little Butch."

I smiled. I think I liked it, too.

"Then, Little Butch, we need to negotiate a contract so you know what you can expect and what's expected of you. We'll spell everything out so there'll be no misunderstandings. Agreed?"

I nodded. Somehow, it made sense.

Helen took out a pad of paper and began to jot down some notes. "There's usually an advocate to take your side. Do you want one?"

"Do I need one?" That didn't sound right. My stomach started to turn. This was harder than having a booking agent to find performance jobs.

"Not if you don't want one. You'll have to trust me, though. And seeing that this is your first time and you're untrained, we'll put lots of escape clauses in it."

"Fine with me. I trust you," I said with a nonchalance I didn't know if I felt.

"All right. First, there will be a training period. During that time, everything will be carefully explained to you, how you should act, what you can and cannot say, what you can do, etc. If I am satisfied with your progress, I will extend the contract, making you my full submissive or slave, a full member of my family. If not, I will release you, and you will be free to go your own way. Also, during the training period, if you cannot or decide you don't want to adhere to the rules of the training, you may break the contract." She looked at me for agreement.

"How long will the training period be?"

"Until you learn what I think you should know. If you train as quickly as you did last night, it shouldn't take long at all." Her smile warmed me. I had the feeling that somehow, this was the right thing. For the first time that day, I felt the same surety and desire I'd felt last night.

She reached down and ran her fingers through my hair, stopping to caress my cheek. "I have the feeling that this is right for you. Perhaps enjoy will become the right word."

"Perhaps," I said. "I think I did enjoy most of last night."

Helen smiled broadly. "I thought you did. Now, terms of the contract. This will be an exclusive contract. You will not sleep, have sex, or whatever you want to call it, with anyone else without either my permission or my request. In fact, you will not even talk with anyone unless you have my permission. Is that understood? That part is not negotiable."

I nodded happily. At that moment, I didn't want to be with anyone but her.

"During your training period, you will be required to perform certain acts with Neisy. And that is also not negotiable. She is a part of my family right now and is bound to me by the same type of contract. Shall we continue?"

I thought it over. I didn't really want to have sex with Neisy, but if it brought me closer to Helen, well, maybe... "All right."

"In exchange," she continued, "I will train you and provide you with food and lodging and an allowance to buy necessities. This, of course, has nothing to do with the contract we negotiated about your work with my music. That contract is totally different and is still in force. You, in reality, will do whatever I ask of you, without question. You will turn over all conscious decision making to me. I will guide you in all ways, and you will seek my advice and consent in everything. And you will be rewarded in many different ways for work done well...or disciplined for errors. Of course, to those outside this apartment, it will look like you merely work for me. You will be introduced to strangers as my personal assistant. Do I make myself clear?"

"Yes," I answered firmly. I was ready at that moment to sign my life away to this woman. I was amazed that I was ready to sign my life over to her...but there was always a way out, wasn't there?

She stopped.

"Training lesson number one," she said. "You will always address me and others with terms of respect. You'll say yes, ma'am, or no, ma'am, or you'll call me mistress. You'll never be bold enough to presume you can call me Helen. When we're in public or there are other people around, you will call me Miss Robins. Is that clear?"

"Yes, ma'am."

She smiled again. "Good boy. Do you drink?"

"Do you mean alcohol? I have some rum and ginger every once in a while."

"Well, you won't. You have to keep your mind very clear. You have to know when to use your safe word. You can't let yourself get out of control, even if you think you can handle it. Accidents happen when someone is not sharp or too inebriated to make the right choices. I'll let you know when I think you can handle a drink. Am I clear?"

"Yes, ma'am."

"Now, next point of the contract…"

The rest of the negotiation took about two hours. She asked me about my background, my family, my fears and hopes, my likes and dislikes, Finally, she had me read the list of terms she'd written, and I signed my agreement and consent. She initialed beneath my name and set the paper back on her desk.

"You can have a copy of this made for yourself when you go to the copy service. And you can move your belongings into the room next to Neisy's."

I thought of the two rooms beyond the kitchen which had once been maids' quarters. Neisy and I would share the small bathroom back there.

"Where have you been staying?" Helen asked.

"The Hotel Earle in the Village."

"That roach trap?" Helen cried. "Go and get your things out of there immediately and shake them out thoroughly. I won't have you bringing bugs into this apartment! Better still, just drop everything off at the cleaners on the corner. I'll call and have your name added to my account. Go, but don't take all day. You still have a lot of work to do on this music. I'll have Neisy leave out some fresh linen for you."

She watched as I got to my feet. "Yes, ma'am." I saluted her with a crisp military swagger.

"And don't start any of that Mickey Mouse Club silliness. If you mouth off too much, it could get you into a lot of hot water! But then, maybe you'd enjoy that, too." Her smile was unsettling. I couldn't determine if that was good or bad. "Just don't push me."

I hesitated. All at once, thousands of questions were racing through my mind. "Mistress?" I started. The appellation still felt foreign to my tongue.

"Speak."

I wasn't quite sure what I wanted to ask. "How did you know about me? I mean, what made you think I'd go for this, that I'd be good at it? I mean, why me?"

Helen studied me. "In this lifestyle, you learn to judge people's body language. I watched you. I looked in your eyes. You wanted to be with me that night at the party after the concert, but you were too tentative. I could have snapped my fingers, and you'd have been there at my side. Am I right?"

I had to admit the truth.

"At first, I wasn't sure, but last night, when you walked into the dungeon, well, the look in your eyes as you stared at Neisy was wonderful. I knew right then that I might never get you out of there. You just looked natural…scared but natural." She chuckled, then looked back at me. "And I asked Andrew certain questions about you. He said that you were a talented musician, but you needed direction and that you liked to mouth off quite a bit."

I shrugged.

"He also said you were lovers with his cousin. She was one of the singers in that vocal group, wasn't she? Which one?"

"The alto."

Helen seemed to consider this. "Not bad; you have good taste, but she's way below your league."

"We just broke up."

"I know. Andrew said that would probably happen."

"Does Andrew know what I'm doing here?" I was suddenly very scared that Andrew knew all about what was happening here.

"My God, no!" Helen glared. "That vanilla boy would never understand any of this. He thinks I want to hire you as a rehearsal pianist." She laughed. "You don't have to worry. I'm sure that no one in your sweet little Boston circle has the slightest idea about what happens in this apartment. Or if they did, they'd be so scandalized they'd swallow their tongue rather than talk about it! No, my dear Little Butch, I'm very discreet, especially when I'm making inquiries about possible slaves. I've had to be, or this would have been out long ago. Now, have I settled your fears, or do you have other questions?"

I thought. "How will I know what's right or wrong? I mean, how will I know each and every time if I'm overstepping the boundaries?"

She looked at me thoughtfully. "You'll learn. Some by training, such as calling me Mistress. Other times by trial and error. The first error will be corrected; the second time it happens will be disciplined. If you start acting out just to get my attention or mouthing off because you enjoy the discipline, I'll stop you. Don't try to mouth your way around here, Mickey." She thought for a minute. "In fact, that will be my safe word. If you're crossing the line or getting on my nerves, I'll call you Mickey Mouth. That will be your cue to stop."

"Mickey Mouth?" I asked incredulously.

She smiled. "It just seems to fit, doesn't it? Now go, before I change my mind, Mickey Mouth."

"Yes, ma'am." I grinned and was on my way out the door.

❖

As I threw my clothes into the suitcase, it hit me. I'd just signed myself into slavery.

I'd never been the one to align myself with any one teacher, only one mentor. I'd taken all I could from each and every resource, sorted through it, and chosen what I felt was right for me. I'd always been the one to hedge all bets, never going steady or making a commitment to one lover. I'd never been faithful. Why had I just devoted my life, my work, and my body to this one woman?

Of course, it was Helen Robins.

I sat on the bed as I folded a shirt. Was it the sex? And why was I even considering these alternatives?

I closed my eyes and took a deep breath. What had come over me? Even now, eighty blocks away, I could feel the pull. I wanted to get back. Why? So she could beat my butt until I couldn't sit? Was I that much of a masochist? So she could correct the way I played the piano? So I could grovel at her feet?

I shook myself as if from a bad dream.

But the feeling as she'd touched me, as she'd held me in her arms, as she'd kissed my neck sent shivers through me. Just how much had the paddling turned me on? I tried to analyze the feelings.

I'd never wanted anyone the way I wanted Helen Robins. I'd always wanted her. I remembered falling asleep at night listening to her records, making love to her music, even masturbating to it. Was this what I'd been training myself for all this time?

Thinking back to the night I'd first seen her onstage, I'd known I wanted to be with her. At the party, I'd wanted her. Over the phone, I'd wanted to be with her. Now I had the chance. Even that short scene last night had been what I'd wanted. I could still feel her hands on me, in me. It had felt like a dream coming true.

But on what terms? The ones she'd set forth this morning? The ones that said I would serve her every whim and maybe, only maybe, earn the chance of touching her, hugging her? Neisy had said I'd never make love to Helen, that no one touched Helen, that she only took her pleasure from the pain and pleasure of others.

No, I vowed. I wanted a lover, someone who could receive as well as give. I wanted to kiss and nuzzle and caress. No stone butches need apply. I could just hop a train back to Boston and be out of here tonight. I didn't have to go back. Helen could send me the tapes if she still wanted me to transcribe them or just send me the money she already owed me, and I'd be done. No! Damn it, I wasn't going to be a slave to anyone. I was not going back to the Upper West Side.

I slammed the shirt into the suitcase.

Of course, this was Helen Robins.

I started to shake. My whole body ached with longing. I wanted Helen to touch me again. I wanted to see that smile on her face that said, "You please me, my Little Butch." Even the soreness on my butt felt good because it had pleased Helen to make it that way.

Damn. What was wrong with me? What had I become?

I glanced into the wavy mirror over the rickety old chest of drawers in the shabby hotel room. "Okay," I asked myself, "which will it be? Boston or the Upper West Side? Marlboros or Shermans?"

Once again, I sank onto the bed.

It seemed like the dream of a lifetime. Helen Robins wanted me. Or was that the nightmare? What did she want of me? Just my body and my musical ears? Or did she want my soul?

Damn, I thought, standing again. *How do I make this decision? Is this the kind of life I want to lead? Am I just doing this because it's Helen? Am I doing it for me?*

Walking. That was what I needed to do. I needed to walk around and think it through. Walking had always been the way I'd made choices. Walking, thinking, walking some more, looking for signs to let me know if I'd chosen right.

The answer was out there in the city, in the Village. Maybe right outside on West Fourth Street. Or down the block in Washington Square. I jammed the room key into my pocket, picked up my suitcase, and closed the door behind me. I'd definitely be sleeping somewhere else tonight.

❖

I'm not sure how far I walked, but my mind was racing. It dawned on me that it all came down to "what do I want to be when I grow up?" Hell, I hadn't thought of that in years. In high school, I'd gone from one idea to another with no direction, then finally decided on being a music teacher. Then in college, a professor suggested that I give up the idea of teaching in public schools and make "theory" my focus, along with some composition and arranging. So without even thinking about it, I'd changed my major. Now where was I going? Toward being a great composer? I thought not. A gifted arranger? Probably not. What did I want to do? What did I want?

The thought scared me. I'd always let fate, or at least another person, make decisions for me. It was easier that way because I didn't have to take any responsibility, could just float though life.

But what did I want? I had no idea.

I kept walking.

Finally, I came up with a short list. I wanted to be a

musician…a pianist. A jazz pianist. And I wanted a relationship. A lasting relationship with one person. Would I have that with Helen? Did I have it in Boston?

The answer to both was a resounding no.

But what did I have in Boston? A dead relationship with Ann and a string of one-night stands. The rest of the time I treaded water playing for voice and dance classes and teaching until I was so tired, I had no time for my own music.

I balanced that against what I'd have in New York: a very alive relationship, sort of, if you didn't consider it one-way, but definitely not a string of one-night stands. I'd be with the same woman, or women, each and every night, for as long as…well, who knew. And I'd be studying the music of the one person in the world I'd dreamed of being like. I wanted to develop my own style and be known in the industry. But at what cost?

I looked around. Somehow, I'd walked thirty blocks without realizing it. I could walk a few more to the train station under Madison Square Garden and be back in Boston before midnight.

My suitcase was getting heavy, and my stomach started to churn at the thought of leaving. *Do I stay, or do I go?* I walked once more around the block.

"Okay, kiddo," I said to myself as I stood in front of the entrance to Madison Square Garden. "Go back to Boston and hope you'll find something safe, or take a big step and stay here in New York with Helen."

I took a very deep breath. The longing to call someone and talk it over washed over me. Maybe I should call Frank.

"No. It's time to be a big girl in the big city. Make your own decisions. Okay, what did Helen say? If I wanted out, I could ask for it anytime. This isn't like a marriage or a lifetime commitment."

Or was it? Last night's sex had been incredible, and I could have that again. All the time? How often did Helen want it? She'd have two of us now, so she must want it frequently.

But she'd make all the decisions. Did I want that? Hadn't I wished that someone would take over once in a while? That someone would think for me, so I could concentrate on my music? Yes. That was exactly what I wanted.

I headed for the subway station that would take me back uptown.

❖

It was dark when I arrived at Helen's. I knew the moment I turned the key in the lock, heard Helen's cough from the music studio, and saw Neisy's face that I'd been gone much too long. I left my suitcase in the entryway and went to the piano. Helen didn't look up from her copy of *Variety*. I waited in the doorway.

"Do you want to be released from your contract?" she asked, not looking up.

I sank to my knees in front of her. "Oh no, ma'am," I said with urgency. "I wasn't sure, but I am now."

She slowly looked down at me.

"I walked around, thinking about it. I've always walked when I have to make a decision. I had to be sure."

"And now you are?" she asked.

"Oh yes, ma'am."

She studied me for a moment, then nodded. Finally, she smiled. "Good. When we start, there's got to be no question in your mind. If we stop, that's it. There'll be no stopping and starting."

"Yes, ma'am."

"And you won't need to walk around anymore. When you

need a decision, I'll give it to you." She chuckled in a way that made me a bit scared. Was she going to punish me? Please? "I suppose I should punish you for making me worry."

"Yes, ma'am." I lowered my eyes to the floor, not wanting her to see the fear or hope.

"What should that punishment be, do you think?"

"Whatever you wish, ma'am."

"Should I spank you?" she said with a smile in her voice.

"If you'd like, ma'am," I answered, holding my breath. No, she knew I wanted to be punished. The worst punishment would be not being punished.

After a well-timed silence, she asked "Have you had dinner?"

"No, ma'am."

There was silence again. Finally, I peeked to see what she was thinking. She sat in her chair, holding a Sherman. Her look insinuated that there was something I needed to do. Smiling, I reached for her lighter and held the flame for her. Finally, after a long inhale and a brief cough, she looked at me.

"Well, my boy, Neisy has been holding dinner. I think we should eat now and get a good night's sleep. There's a lot to be done tomorrow. And I think you're much too willing to be punished."

"Yes, ma'am." I smiled.

"But," she started, pointing, "you will not cause me to worry again. If you are detained, you will call. If you have questions, you will tell me. Is that clear? I don't want to be your mother, but I won't be left hanging, not knowing where you are. This is New York City. This is a dangerous place. Do you understand?"

"Yes, ma'am. I'm sorry I didn't call. I…"

She held up her hand to stop me. "You have a phone with you?"

"Yes, ma'am."

"You will code this number into it immediately."

"Yes, ma'am."

"Enough. That was the first time you erred. It will be the last. I'm very sure of that. Aren't you?"

"Yes, ma'am."

"Then go tell Neisy we're ready for dinner."

Chapter Five

Dinner was good: broiled pork chops, Helen's favorite; rice; and green beans. Neisy was a good cook, nothing fancy but tasty and well prepared.

For dessert, Neisy brought out éclairs she'd gotten at a local bakery. Helen seemed pleased by them.

It felt like a family. Helen held the place at the head of the table, Neisy and me on either side of her like sisters, me the younger, although I had the feeling I was a couple years older than Neisy. I watched my manners and tried to fit in.

As she finished eating, Helen looked at me. "You will do the cleaning after meals. Neisy does the cooking, and you will do the dishes. You can share the rest of the responsibilities."

"Yes, ma'am."

"Neisy, take it upon yourself to explain things to the boy."

"With pleasure, Mistress."

As we rose from the table, Neisy went to the bar and poured a glass of sherry and brought it to Helen, who moved to her black leather chair, again reading *Variety*. It seemed like a comfortable evening after dinner in the average American household.

As Neisy helped me clean, showing me where everything belonged, she told me about Helen's likes and dislikes.

"She drinks vodka with a splash of tonic water and a twist of lemon. Not too much tonic. She likes to taste the vodka." She grinned. "She's also very particular about the quality of the food she eats. Most things we can buy at D'Agostino's around the corner. She has a charge account there. I'll remind her to add your name.

"Meats and produce have to be chosen specially. There are several little produce shops in the area that she likes. And only bread from Zabar's. Never get a regular loaf of white bread. You'll end up eating it…all in one sitting…and without any water." She laughed as if speaking from personal experience. "She loves chocolate but not too much of it. And always broiled food, never fried.

"She can get on a health food kick and drink nothing but gallons of that damned carrot and celery juice for days, or she'll open a bottle of sherry and drink half of it before she goes to bed. She's a woman of extremes. Nothing is ever halfway.

"And those cigarettes! Make sure you keep an eye on how many are left under the bar. Always make sure there's at least three new packs. If the supply gets low, call Nat Sherman's over on Fifth Avenue, and they'll deliver. She's one of the few who have them make those eight-inch things. Don't ever let her run out, or there'll be hell to pay."

Neisy went on and on until I thought my head would split open. So many little details. How would I ever remember them all?

As we finished, Neisy showed me where the linens were kept. I made my bed, unpacked my few possessions, and started to settle in.

Neisy beckoned from the door. "Come say good night," she whispered. "Always check with her before you go to bed."

I followed her to the living room.

"We've finished, Mistress," Neisy began when Helen finally acknowledged our presence. "Is there anything you'd like before we turn in?"

Helen looked at each of us. "Are you settled in?" she asked me.

"Pretty much, ma'am," I answered, remembering my manners. "I still have things at the cleaners."

"Well, if you need anything, just let Neisy know. She'll tell you where to get it. Get a good night's sleep. Both of you. We have a lot of work to do tomorrow."

"Good night, Mistress," Neisy said as she crept over to Helen. Helen raised her cheek, and Neisy planted a soft kiss there, then disappeared into her bedroom. I hesitated. Was that the way I was supposed to kiss Helen good night, too?

"Questions, Little Butch?" Helen asked.

"I'm just not sure of the protocol," I said softly.

Helen smiled. "If I want to kiss something, then I will, but I dislike being kissed on the mouth," she stated flatly. "If you wish, you can kiss my cheek or my hand." She smiled evilly. "Or my shoe, if that makes you happy."

I could feel myself start to blush. "Not tonight, if it pleases you, Mistress, ma'am," I whispered in my most submissive tone, trying to keep a stupid grin off my face.

"Watch yourself, Mickey Mouth, that's getting close."

I smiled, planted a quick kiss on her cheek, and went into my room. This would take some getting used to. As I settled down between the crisp white sheets of my new bed, it hit me. I was living with Helen Robins. The Helen Robins. And I was more than just working for her. I was…what? Her lover? Her playmate? Her toy? As I started to drift off to sleep, I thought of Frank and Ann in Boston. If they only knew.

❖

The next night, as Helen was getting up from the dinner table, she stopped and looked at both of us. "Nine o'clock. Sharp," was her only comment before she walked up the stairs toward her bedroom.

I looked at Neisy, who had a huge smile across her face.

"Does that..." I wasn't sure I read the comment right, but Neisy nodded.

"We'd better hurry and get ready. This is something you don't want to be late for." She began clearing the table.

"But does that mean..."

"We have to be ready in the dungeon when she gets there at nine o'clock on the button. You don't want to be late or look like you've rushed in. That's important. Always be there ahead of time. And get there early if you need a shower. At least this time it's just nine o'clock. When she really means business, it's never a round number." She studied me. "Looks like your training starts tonight, Little Butch." She drew my name out in a mocking tone but smiled and laughed. "I can't wait to see this. You're gonna love it. Now, remember your manners. It's the proper attitude that will please her. And remember to always say thank you."

"Thank you? For what?"

"For each time she allows you to please her. Each stroke of her whip, each slap of her hand is a gift from her. Let her know that you're grateful for her allowing you to please her and for being here."

I had to stop and consider that. Grateful that she abused me? Or grateful that she allowed me to feel the pain of her love? Or grateful that she gave me such incredible orgasms? This was weird, but I could get used to it.

I followed her into the kitchen with my arms full of dishes and my stomach protesting the extra cup of coffee I'd had. I took a deep breath to try and quiet it, but my stomach had decided to do calisthenics, and nothing could settle it.

❖

At nine o'clock, both Neisy and I were kneeling in the middle of the dungeon, naked, our backs to the door when I heard it open.

"Nice." Helen's voice sighed as she entered. "I see that Neisy has given you good instructions to start. That's very good." She stalked toward us, but the sound of my own heartbeat threatened to drown out every other sound.

"Neisy, you will assist me tonight. You may stand."

"Thank you, Mistress," Neisy said as she got up. I started to let myself settle onto my heels, but a sharp rap on the shoulder stopped me.

"Don't get comfortable, Little Butch, we're just beginning." Helen's voice was close behind me, over my shoulder.

"This will be your first lesson, but it will be the most important one. The main thing you need to learn is control. In all things, you will never be in control of the situation except for one very important aspect: yourself. You must learn to control your actions and your reactions. You must learn to control your own pacing. You must learn to control your mind and your body. That's where we'll start tonight. Now, crawl to that corner."

I stared.

"Don't ever look a domina in the eye unless she tells you to," she warned, her eyes narrowing. "Keep your eyes lowered in respect. Looking your domina in the eye makes her think you're challenging her. Don't even think of challenging a command."

I had to think about that. Why would I balk at a command?

"That can get you in very deep trouble. Now, get on all fours and crawl to that platform in the corner." Her voice was stern but not cold. I knew I could do what she asked. I crawled to the far wall and up onto the eight-inch-tall platform built into the corner of the room.

"Now stand up."

I got to my feet and started to turn toward her.

Her sharp, "Did I tell you to turn around?" stopped me.

"No, ma'am," I whispered and faced the wall.

"Good. Now turn around."

I understood. *Don't think, just obey to the letter. Okay, if these are the rules…* I turned to face her.

"Raise your hands over your head." I looked at her. She slapped my face, not gently, but without much force. "Why are you looking at me?"

I lowered my eyes. "I'm sorry, Mistress."

"Not good enough. Admit your transgression. Then ask for forgiveness. Humbly. With the right amount of respect." She took a step back and waited.

I swallowed. This was tougher than I thought. "I'm sorry I looked in your eyes, Mistress," I stammered, trying to find the right words. "It was stupid and rude of me. I wouldn't think of questioning your requests. I ask for your forgiveness."

"Ask? You should beg for my forgiveness."

"I beg your forgiveness."

I waited, praying she'd accept that. "This time I will forgive you," she said after what seemed like an hour. "But the next time, there will be a price to pay for your transgression."

"Yes, ma'am," I said, keeping my eyes on the floor.

"Now raise your hands above your head." She waited as

I reached above me. Out of the corner of my eye, I saw Neisy taking some equipment from the armoire. Then, Neisy came over and pulled two chains down from the ceiling to shackle my hands.

She took out a flat metal bar about four feet long with leather cuffs chained to each end. Kneeling in front of me, she buckled the cuffs to each of my ankles. My legs were spread wide apart. It was a little disturbing that I couldn't move my feet, that my legs were stretched. I swallowed. If this was what Helen wanted... Then she went to the wall and pulled the chains attached to my wrists up through the pulleys on the ceiling until I was stretched to my full height. I felt like a target. There was no way to move, except my chest pumped in and out as my breathing started escalating.

"That's very nice. Very nice indeed," Helen said, pacing up to me. "Do you remember what we talked about yesterday?"

"Yes, ma'am."

"Then you remember that you belong to me, and you'll do anything I say. Is that correct?"

"Yes, ma'am."

"You remember that you pledged to please me?"

"Yes, ma'am."

"I could leave you here, just like this for days if I wanted, and you wouldn't protest?"

"No, ma'am." I was starting to feel a little scared that she wasn't just playing with my head.

"No, I can't leave you here or no, you won't protest?"

"No, ma'am, I wouldn't protest." Was I starting to sweat?

She hesitated. My breathing quickened. "Relax, Little Butch." Helen laughed, caressing my face. "I have no intention of leaving you here." She stopped. "This time." There was a sinister edge to her voice. "We have more important things to do tonight. Neisy, bring me the clamps."

Neisy handed her some small alligator clamps held together by a thin silver chain.

Helen stepped close to me and ran her hand over my chest.

"You have very nice breasts," she said. "And wonderful nipples. So dark and large. I think this will work just fine." As she spoke, she ran her hands over my breasts, stopping at each nipple to coax it to erection. A series of tremors ran through my body as she rolled each one between her fingers.

"You like having your nipples touched, don't you, boy?" she said, almost through her teeth.

"Yes, Mistress," I sighed, beginning to feel the heat rise between my legs.

"It turns you on, doesn't it?" Her touch became harder as she pinched.

"Yes, Mistress." My breath was already a little ragged. What was she going to do?

"Excellent. This pleases me very much." Her pinching began to get harder and harder. "You do want to please me, don't you, boy?"

"Yes, ma'am." All I wanted right then was to touch my nipples and rub the teasing away. It was becoming unsettling.

"And this hurts, but you enjoy it, don't you, because it pleases me." Her grasp on my nipples had gotten tighter and tighter.

"Yes, ma'am." I knew I could get through this. Couldn't I? It was what she wanted me to do, and that made me want it even more.

"Then this will feel even better." She placed the clamps, one on each of my nipples, and tightened them until the pain made my eyes water. "Are these too tight?" she asked.

"Yes, ma'am." I was breathing shallowly, trying to keep my chest from moving.

"I don't think so. I can make them tighter. See?" She gave

the screw on each clamp an extra quarter turn. I gasped as the pain shot through me. "You do enjoy this pain, don't you? Because it pleases me very much."

"Yes, ma'am," I moaned, not quite sure I meant what I was saying.

"Excellent. Now let's see what we can add. Neisy?"

Neisy handed her something, then stepped back. Helen held out a small copper cowbell and hung it on the chain that connected the two clamps. As she let it drop, its weight pulled on the clamps, and pain shot through me. I gasped as the bell rang loudly.

"Does that hurt?" she asked.

"Yes, ma'am," I stammered, trying to keep the tears in my eyes from falling.

"Very much?"

"Yes, ma'am."

"I shouldn't think it would, but I guess we'll find out, won't we?"

"Yes, ma'am." I sighed, giving up all hope that this would end soon. The pain was so constant that it was beginning to have a strange effect. If I forced my concentration away, I could almost ignore it. I looked at the floor, trying to estimate how far it was to the door. Anything to keep my mind occupied. I had to survive this without letting Helen down. I was handling it better than I thought I could. I couldn't imagine what I was experiencing. Now, if I could reach that point where the pain spilled over into pleasure.

"Now, here's the catch," Helen said. "We don't want that bell to ring. And only you can keep it from ringing. See, if you move too quickly"—she pushed my shoulder, and I jerked backward, pain shooting through my nipples and the bell ringing loudly—"or if you breathe too deeply"—I gasped as she pinched my nipple, and the bell rang—"the bell will ring.

Now, we don't want it to ring because each time it does, I'll have to swat your rear with one of my instruments, and that would be very painful."

I had to force myself not to look at her.

"So you see, you do have control of this situation, don't you? You can choose to allow the bell to ring or not, can't you?"

I breathed in a slow, long sigh, trying to keep my chest still. "Yes, ma'am," I managed.

Helen laughed. "Good boy. But now, I have another little game to play."

She reached between my legs and ran her hand across my clit. I inhaled sharply as my clit jumped under her touch. The bell rang.

"Not a good start, boy, but we won't start counting until I'm ready. You see, you have to understand the rules of the game. You're very hot and wet down here, so you're ready to play, and I love the feel of it, so I'm ready to play, but there always have to be rules to a game, don't there?" She waited.

My mind was racing. What was she going to do? "Yes, ma'am. If you want them, ma'am."

"Good boy. You see, the object of this game is for me to play with your clit until you come. But you won't allow me to make you come until I've finished my cigarette because if I have a lit cigarette in my hand when you come, you're not sure what I'll do with it." I could sense evilness and a deep enjoyment in her voice. Fear raced through me. I could feel its effect in my cunt. "Besides, coming right away takes all the fun out of the game. It ends things much too soon unless you can come again and again and again. Can you?" She squeezed my breast roughly.

"I don't know, Mistress. I've never actually counted." I gasped and had to hold my breath to keep from shaking.

Helen chuckled. "Then I guess you'll have to learn to control it. Now for the game. You have two objectives: one, not to come until my cigarette is finished, and two, not to let the bell ring because then I'll have to punish you. Now, do you understand the rules of the game?"

"Yes, ma'am," I whispered softly, trying not to move.

"Good. Then let's begin." I watched as Neisy handed her one of her eight-inch Shermans and held a lighter for her. Helen took a deep drag on the cigarette, then reached into my crotch with her other hand.

At first, her fingers just probed and explored, but then a fingernail scratched my clit, and I jumped at the unexpected sensation. The bell rang.

"Not a good start, boy, unless you enjoyed the other night more than I thought," Helen said. "I know you can do better than that."

"Yes, ma'am," I whispered with my eyes closed.

"Good boy," Helen said in her warmest voice. "Then let's continue."

Her fingers began their exploration again, returning time after time to my hardened clit. She massaged it gently, and I could feel the tension starting to build. I looked up at the chains attached to my wrists. *Maybe I should count the links, maybe that will keep my mind off this.*

Then Helen's fingers dove deeply into me. I gasped. The bell rang. Then her fingers were back on my clit, massaging it very gently as if it was like a feather. Without looking at her, I could sense the evil in her demeanor. She wasn't going to make this easy, was she?

She rolled my clit between her thumb and finger. Next, she'd run her finger around and around the edge, ever so lightly. The sensations were incredible. I looked at her cigarette. Not even an inch had burned away. How would I get through this? My body was already beginning to feel the surge of an oncoming climax.

But then, Helen stopped touching me. My body, already adjusted to the probing, wasn't ready to be abandoned. It wanted more. It wanted to be touched and fondled.

"Please, Mistress," I whimpered, "please." The bell rang.

"Oh, I haven't stopped, Little Butch. I was just flicking my ash away. There'll be more. Lots more." With that, she returned her hand to my wetness. Her touch, so gentle and light, was beginning to drive me crazy. My body was crying out to be touched, touched hard, fucked. Not just feather-brushed. I wanted to push into her hand, but it was always just on the edge of my reach.

I must have whimpered. The bell rang.

"Is there something you want, boy?" Helen asked.

"Yes, ma'am," I answered, careful not to move for fear that the bell would ring again.

"What do you want, Little Butch?"

I was beside myself. Couldn't she tell what I needed? Why was she holding back? "Touch me, please."

"I am touching you. Ever so lightly, right here." Her finger made a circle around my clit.

"Harder, please."

"Are you telling me what to do?"

I squeezed my eyes shut. "Oh no, ma'am. I'd never tell you what to do."

"That's good, because you can't tell me what to do. You know that, don't you, boy?"

"Yes, ma'am."

"And why is that?"

"Because you're in control. You are the Mistress."

"Good." I could sense her smile. "Do you still want me to touch you harder?"

I was about to lose it. I nodded.

She grabbed my face and lifted it. I had to keep my eyes shut to keep from looking into her face. "What?"

"Yes, ma'am."

"And risk you coming before my cigarette is finished? I don't think that would be wise, boy."

My body trembled. I heard the bell, but I didn't care. My body was crying out to be touched. I didn't know how much longer I could take her teasing. I looked at her cigarette. It was only half gone. "Please, just a little harder, ma'am? Just a little, please, Mistress?"

"What do you think, Neisy? Should I put him out of his misery? Or make him wait like a good boy?"

"Make him wait, Mistress," Neisy said, her voice husky and breathy. "It will teach him respect."

"I agree. He needs to learn respect. He's much too bold. Much, much too bold."

Her fingers continued their circling at an ever-so-slow pace, barely touching me, but the sensations continued to unnerve me. I started to quiver and heard a ring.

"He must like being lashed, don't you think, Neisy? That bell rings quite a bit, doesn't it?"

"He's never felt the lash, ma'am," Neisy said. "Maybe he doesn't know what he's in for." Her laughter rang in my ears.

"Well, Little Butch, I know you're trying hard to control yourself, but you'll have to try even harder. I can't make this cigarette burn any faster."

I looked at the ceiling. "I'm trying, ma'am," I managed to say between shallow breaths as my body threatened to explode.

"I know, boy. This is a hard lesson, isn't it?"

"Yes, ma'am." The strokes were incredible, almost reaching that thin line that divided the pain from the pleasure.

I was right on that tigh rope, ready to tumble into the pleasure, yet fully aware of the pain. God. Would this ever end?

The stroking continued. In my head, I counted the links of chain, recited the names of all the toys hanging in the armoire. I even searched the wallpaper for seams to count so I had some way to steady my concentration and control what was threatening to erupt. I'd never had to have this much control in my whole life.

Finally, I heard, "Look at my cigarette, boy."

I opened my eyes and watched with joy as she ground it out in the ashtray Neisy held. As soon as she'd snuffed all the sparks, she drove her hand into my cunt.

I exploded. Wave after wave of incredible orgasm poured out of me. I heard the bell ringing somewhere in the distance, but I didn't care. I was too awash in sensations, the tensions in my muscles too intense.

I felt her arm around me. She held me close as her other hand worked its magic in my crotch. I let myself fall forward, laying my head against her shoulder.

"Such a good Little Butch," she whispered into my hair. "You please me, boy. You please me a great deal."

I leaned into her, trying to catch my breath. "Thank you, ma'am." Neisy released my ankles from their cuffs, and I staggered to hold myself up.

"Take a moment," Helen cautioned. "Enjoy it while you can."

I drew a deep ragged breath as she pushed me back up on my own. My hands were still shackled, and that was the only thing that kept me from falling on my face.

"I don't think we'll need these anymore."

I looked down just in time to see her take the clamps from my nipples. The world exploded, and I was engulfed in white lightning as pain shot through me. I screamed as the blood rushed back into the crushed skin and the numbed flesh jumped to life again. Helen hugged me close, her warm, strong embrace the only reality in my sea of sensations as the pain morphed into feelings that blended the pain and pleasure.

I passed out for a moment and felt a gentle, cool, wet towel being wiped across my face. As the pain subsided, I let myself hang from the ceiling, my mind completely blank. I couldn't remember my name.

After a few minutes, Neisy loosened the chains, and I stumbled to remain standing as the chains lowered, and she released my wrists from the shackles. I grabbed my breasts and rubbed my nipples.

When I at last looked up, Helen was seated on her stool, watching me. "Very good, boy." She smiled at me. "Very, very good."

I melted under her approval and leaned back against the wall, still gasping for air. "Thank you, Mistress." I grinned. I'd passed my first test.

But then she stood. "Now, there's only the matter of the ringing bell."

Oh shit, I'd forgotten. Could I fall on my knees and beg for leniency?

She must have read my mind. "You can't avoid it. It was part of the deal. For every time the bell rang, you get your ass walloped. Wasn't that part of the rules?"

"Yes, ma'am," I whispered, my mind racing in several directions, trying to figure out how to get out of this. The only escape I knew was to use my safe word and walk out, but then, I'd be lost. I'd never have those feelings from Helen again.

She stepped onto the platform, took me by the back of the neck, and led me to the center of the floor. "Now, you've felt this paddle, so it shouldn't be a surprise even though this one may feel harder. But we'll try it a little differently. This time, you won't have the horse or my lap to lean against. You'll have to keep yourself standing." She took the paddle from Neisy. "There are other rules for this, so listen carefully." She leered. "If you touch something to steady yourself, we add another lash. If your knee touches the floor, we add two more, or if you fall to the ground, we start all over again. Do you have any questions?"

I looked in fear at Neisy, hoping that there'd be something she could do to help, but she just laughed. "I think you'd better start before he dies of fright."

"Okay, then." Helen sneered. "Bend over. You can place your hands on your knees if it'll help you balance, but be very careful. You don't want to fall, do you?"

"No, ma'am," I stammered. "I mean, yes, ma'am. I mean, I'd better not fall…" At that moment, the panic was so intense that I wasn't really sure what I meant to say. I put my hands on my knees and tried to calm my breathing, but my mind focused back on the feel of Helen's hands touching me.

"Now, let's see, how many times did the bell ring? Were either of you keeping count?"

I looked a Neisy. I hadn't been keeping track. "Six or seven?" Neisy said.

"I would have guessed twelve or fifteen," was Helen's answer. "What did you count, boy?"

I tried to swallow, but my mouth was so dry, I could barely force my lips into words. "Six?"

Helen just laughed. "I think the two of you are in a conspiracy here. I know it was more than six, but since I can't prove it, I'll compromise. Let's say eight."

I looked up at Neisy. "Thank her," she mouthed.

"Yes, eight would be right, ma'am. Thank you very much, Mistress."

The very first slap of the lash stunned me and sent me

flying forward. I struggled to maintain my balance, and it was only at the last moment that I didn't grab the padded bench as I stumbled toward it.

"Get back here."

I staggered back to the place in front of her and bent over once again.

The second, third, and fourth slaps hurt even more, but I was determined to keep my balance even though my knees were starting to weaken. I was gasping for breath as I bent over for the fifth. This time, when the lash struck, my knees buckled, and I touched the floor to keep from falling. I looked down to make sure my knee hadn't touched.

"That will make number nine," Helen said with too much joy in her voice.

"Yes, Mistress," I gasped. "Thank you."

I was determined not to let it happen again, so I braced myself. Tears ran down my face, but I sniffed back a sob as the sixth one hit. My ass was on fire. It was much worse than the previous night, and on top of it, I had to concentrate to stay on my feet.

The seventh hit me a little lower than the others, and I stumbled again, losing my balance and touching the floor.

"That's ten," Helen said. "You must really like this."

"Yes, ma'am, thank you." Before I could brace myself again, the eighth one sent me stumbling to my knees.

"That makes it an even dozen. Right, boy?"

"Yes, ma'am. An even dozen," I managed between sobs. I'd show Helen that I was worth it, that I could be her boy, and I *would* get through this.

"I'll make it easy on you, seeing this is your first lesson. While you're on your hands and knees, crawl to the armoire and bring me the short black switch. Carry it in your mouth."

I glanced up at Neisy, who stood looking at Helen with

great concern. "Do you think he's ready for that?" she asked hesitantly.

Helen turned to her. "Would you rather take this for him? We can start at number one if you feel like questioning me."

Neisy took a step back. "Oh no, Mistress. I would never question you. I was just concerned that he might not be able to please you as much as you wish. He is new."

"Yes, he's new," Helen said. "But he learns fast and wants to please me so much. Don't you, boy?"

"Oh, yes, ma'am," I said. "I'll learn fast." I'd do whatever she asked because I wanted to please her.

"Then get me the switch."

I crawled to the armoire as quickly as I could without causing my ass to burn even more. I looked inside, trying to remember which one was the right switch.

"Show him," Helen commanded.

Neisy reached for the slender rod and held it out so that I could take it between my teeth. I crawled back to Helen.

"Seeing this is your first time, I'll make it even easier. You won't have to stand. Put your head on the floor, but keep your ass as high as you can."

"Yes, ma'am. Thank you, ma'am," I said, leaning to the floor.

Helen paced behind me. "Now, how many have we had so far?"

"Eight, ma'am."

"And how many in all?"

"Twelve, ma'am."

"Just twelve?"

"Yes, please." I was beside myself. Was this torture part of the lesson?

I could see her black shoes pacing.

"So how many are left?"

"Four, ma'am."

Before I could brace myself, the rod bit into my ass. I howled in pain and gasped for breath. The pain spread up my body and into my head.

"Was that right?" Helen asked.

"Yes, Mistress," I managed between sobs. "Thank you."

"So that leaves three?"

Why was she torturing me with these questions? Why not just get it over with? "Yes, ma'am, Three more, please."

"Such a good little boy. Neisy, did you hear how grateful and appreciative he is?"

"Yes, Mistress," Neisy murmured.

"And only three more? Don't you want an extra one, Little Butch?"

"Only three more, please, ma'am." I was breathing hard as the tears fell. I wanted to yell, "Hit me and get it over with," but something told me not to.

The next two came in rapid succession. My whole body was on fire. Sweat poured down my face, and I was having a hard time concentrating. My mind disintegrated into a little pile around my knees. I didn't feel the floor or the air. I floated in a bubble filled with sound and sensations. I was shaking uncontrollably. The wait for the last one seemed interminable.

The last one hit me below my butt, at the top of my thighs, and just grazed my clit. My body erupted. I wasn't sure if I was coming or if the pain so engulfed me that I'd soared to another reality. Whatever it was, pleasure or pain or a combination, it was incredible.

The next thing I knew, Neisy was sitting beside me on the floor, wiping my bruised butt with a cool, wet towel. I was sprawled facedown.

"Are you awake, Little Butch?" Helen asked, kneeling beside me.

"Yes, ma'am." I could feel her caress on my back. She sat on the floor and pulled me into her lap. I buried my face in her thigh and let the tears flow. My butt still burned.

"You're not getting snot all over my clothes, are you?"

"No, ma'am." Neisy handed me the towel, and I wiped the tears and sweat from my face.

"You have pleased me very much tonight, Little Butch. I'm very happy with your progress."

"Thank you, ma'am," I said between sobs.

She curled me into her arms and rocked me gently until my tears subsided. I sank into her embrace, feeling as if my world revolved in these two arms. Her caresses on my back and butt felt like the most soothing balm I could imagine. I'd just committed my life to this wonderful woman. All I wanted was to remain here forever.

When I was finally able to breathe, she took a deep breath and started her next set of instructions. "For the next few days," she began, holding me at arm's length, "you will stay here in this room. You will always be ready for my visits, which will be often and unannounced. You will never stand but will always crawl on your hands and knees. You will sleep under the padded bench, and Neisy will bring your food. You will not speak to her, nor will you refuse to eat what she brings. If I come in here and find that you are not on your hands and knees, I will punish you with a switch much sharper than this. You may use the bathroom when you need to, and you may bathe to get the sweat off and make yourself ready for me, but you will stay here until I release you. There's a blanket in the bottom of the armoire if you get cold. You're not to have any other clothing. Have I made myself clear?"

I glanced at Neisy for reassurance. "Yes, ma'am. I understand. But the music…" I started but bit my lip to keep from questioning her.

"The music can wait a few days. It's not going anywhere. And neither are you. Do you understand?"

"Yes, Mistress."

"Good boy," Helen said as she started to get up. Almost as an afterthought, she added, "I'm very proud of you." With that, she leaned forward and kissed me gently on the mouth.

"Thank you, Mistress," I stammered, not knowing how to react.

Helen got to her feet and offered a hand to Neisy. "Come on, Sweet One, the boy needs his rest."

At the door, Neisy turned back and gave me a thumbs-up. I sat there as the door closed behind them, proudly feeling the ache in my rear. I'd pleased my mistress. And I prayed I could continue to. Why had I ever doubted that decision to stay, the fear I wouldn't please my mistress? I was suddenly overcome with a love for Helen Robins that frightened me with its intensity.

Chapter Six

"Come out here!"

The words woke me from a sound sleep, and I sat up. My head collided with a very low ceiling. It took me a minute to realize where I was, curled up under the padded bench in Helen's dungeon. I crawled out sheepishly, rubbing my head, and looked up into the very amused face of Helen Robins.

"Did I give you permission to abuse yourself?" she asked from her perch on the edge of the bench.

"No, ma'am." I smiled back. "I thought it was you who caused me to bump my head."

She laughed harder. "Yes, I guess it was. Nice comeback."

She circled my neck with her hand, thumb pressing hard against the side of my throat. "Look at me," she ordered as she pulled me almost to my knees. Then she looked deeply into my eyes. "Well, what do you think, Little Butch? Is this what you thought it would be? Are you satisfied or disappointed?" Her gaze unsettled me, and the feel of her strong hand around my throat sent chills down my spine.

"I…I'm not disappointed, Mistress," I stammered, finding it hard to talk and swallow with her hand so tight.

She studied me for another moment before she released her grip. "I just want to make sure you're ready to go on before we take the next step. Are you?"

I felt sweat forming on my upper lip. What was the next step? "Yes, ma'am." I could feel the fear in my voice. My body craved whatever the next step was even if my mind wasn't sure where I fit in.

She held up a handful of leather straps and rope. "Up on your knees. I have some new attire for you."

I straightened on my knees as she handed me a brown leather belt.

"Put this on, the metal loop in the back."

I buckled the belt around my waist and twisted it around me, making sure the silver metal loop was in the center of my back. She then buckled a brown leather collar around my neck.

"Tight enough?" she asked. "Can you still breathe?"

"Yes, ma'am," I answered, feeling the leather at my throat, but it didn't restrict my breathing.

She tied the end of the rope to the collar, then slid the rope between my breasts and through the belt. "Bow your head, chin to chest," she said. "Spread your legs apart."

I bowed my head and widened the space between my knees.

Kneeling, she wound the rope between my legs and up between my ass cheeks. She reached into my crotch, spreading my labia and placing the rope there. Pulling the rope tightly, she knotted it onto the buckle loop at my back.

"There," she smiled, sitting back on her heels. "A new G-string. Now, straighten up."

I gasped as I tried to straighten. As I lifted my head, the rope bit roughly into my clit. There was no way I could straighten without it grinding into me.

Helen got to her feet and towered over me. "That will remind you of the posture you'll need in order to be a good little submissive. Always keep your head bowed and never look up at your mistress. You'll wear this until I allow you to take it off. Waking or sleeping. Am I clear?"

"Yes, ma'am."

"Good, now get some rest. I'll be back soon." She turned to go.

"Mistress…" I started, not moving a muscle.

"What?"

"What if…what if I have to go to the bathroom?" I asked, always thinking of the practical things.

She chuckled that evil laugh that always made me shiver. "I guess you'll find a way, won't you? Just don't take it off." Laughing, she left the room.

I sat there a moment, contemplating how to move without the rope biting into me, then I slowly, carefully, crawled back under the bench and curled up in a fetal position to try to sleep.

❖

I was fully awake but still lying under the bench when I heard the door open. I watched from my cave as bare feet approached.

"Breakfast," Neisy's voice sang as she placed a bowl of cereal and a glass of orange liquid on the floor. "Come on out. You can't hide forever. Helen said I have to watch you eat this."

I crawled out from under the bench, a little rawness between my cheeks.

Neisy broke into laughter when she saw me. "I was wondering if she'd put you in a harness." She smiled, or at least it sounded as if she was smiling. I couldn't raise my head to look without the rope digging into me.

"Don't laugh," I said, reaching for the glass. "Is this her carrot concoction?"

"Oops. You're not supposed to talk to me, remember?" Now it was Neisy's turn to be amused. "She said I could slap you if you did. But seeing as that's only the first time, I'll let it slide."

I sighed deeply and slouched back, trying to relieve some of the tautness in the rope.

"There's no way to get comfortable in that thing, so relax and enjoy it," Neisy said. Was that sympathy I heard? "But eat up, you'll need your strength. Believe me, you'll need all the strength you can get."

I sat in silence, eating the cold cereal and sipping the carrot juice. Thankfully, Neisy had thought to put a straw in the glass. I couldn't have lifted my head to drink if I'd wanted to.

"Would you really slap me if I spoke to you?" I asked, setting the empty glass down on the floor.

Her answer was a sharp slap across my face.

"Yes, I guess you would," I murmured, rubbing my face.

"Just finish your cereal so I can go back downstairs. I think Helen has a few other surprises for you today," Neisy said, picking up the glass. "Oh, and I brought your toothbrush. I'll leave it in the bathroom for you."

"Thanks," I almost said but checked myself before the word was out. Silently, I finished the last two spoonfuls of cereal and handed her the empty dish.

She stood and walked into the bathroom to leave my toothbrush. Then she was gone.

I crawled into the bathroom to try and wash the taste of the carrot juice from my mouth. I'd always liked carrots, but the taste of the celery-flavored juice that early in the morning seemed a little much.

Crawling back out of the bathroom, I tried to raise my head to look at the clock, but that only made the rope tighter, so I sank down in the middle of the floor. I hit a position where the rope pressed but didn't rub my clit. It was almost enjoyable. Moving slightly, I found it very enjoyable indeed. All of the pain and rawness seemed to slip away as I pressed into the rope, grinding back and forth as my body began to heat. I rocked back and forth as the sensations increased.

I must have enjoyed it more than I realized because Helen's voice startled me, and I jumped, causing the rope to bite into my flesh.

"Amazing," she said. "I leave you here to writhe in agony, and you find a way to enjoy it." She laughed deeply. "You are such a brazen hussy, aren't you, my Little Butch? Have you been jacking yourself off all night?"

"No, ma'am," I said, embarrassed that she'd caught me.

"But you are enjoying the harness, aren't you?"

"Just this time, Mistress."

"You are such a slut, aren't you?"

"I guess so, ma'am." What else could I say?

"And enjoying every minute of this bondage, aren't you?"

"Oh no, ma'am," I said, raising my head before I thought about it. The rope reminded me not to move.

"Well you certainly look like you're enjoying it, my little whore. In fact, I suspect that you enjoy the sensations of the pain and pleasure much more than just wanting to please me." As she spoke, she paced slowly, like a panther stalking prey.

"Oh no, Mistress," I said, trying to placate her.

"Are you correcting me?"

"No, Mistress. I couldn't do that. But I like it only because it pleases you."

She stopped so that her blue mules were directly in

front of me. "But you've been rubbing yourself on that rope. Pleasuring yourself without my permission. Did you come?"

"No, ma'am."

"It's a good thing you didn't. There'd be more than four marks across your backside. Or would you enjoy that, too, my Little Butch slut?"

"Oh, Mistress, I wouldn't like that at all." I didn't like the way this conversation was turning. I seemed to be getting deeper into trouble.

She paced several more times in silence. By the time she finally stopped behind me, I could feel the sweat all over my body.

"Why are you afraid?" she asked.

I swallowed. Was I that transparent? "I…I've displeased you, Mistress." It was all I could think to say.

"Oh no, Little Butch," she said. "You haven't displeased me. Not totally because now, at least, I have very good reason to discipline you for your transgression. Don't I?"

"Please, Mistress," I begged, putting my head to the floor as my mind began to buzz with all the possibilities. "Please forgive me. I didn't mean to disobey you."

"Then you admit that you disobeyed me."

Damn, I'd just backed myself into a very uncomfortable corner. "I didn't know it at the time, Mistress."

She answered with a hard smack against my rear. It was painful, especially where I was still sore from last night, but at least it hadn't been the crop.

"Yes, ma'am. Thank you, Mistress," I mumbled, drawing a deep breath.

She straddled me, my body caught between her strong, hard calves. She released the rope. "Stay right where you are, boy," she whispered. "Don't move a muscle."

"Yes, ma'am," I said as she removed the rope from between my legs but left the belt in place.

Her fingers explored my crotch. "You are wet, though, aren't you, boy?" she murmured as her touch glided through me. "You must have really enjoyed pleasuring yourself. Maybe that's something I should see."

I froze as she walked away. I could hear the doors of the armoire open and the sounds of equipment being chosen.

She then knelt directly behind me. "Well, if you enjoy pleasuring yourself so much, maybe that's something that will please me, too," she said, her voice lower, evil. I felt her moving, then something hard pressed against my hole. "Fuck yourself on this, boy." With what could only be that long hard dick Neisy admired so much, she drove into me. I gasped.

"That's it, boy. Don't make me do all the work. Show me how much you can enjoy it." She took hold of the belt and started guiding my body back and forth along the hard rubber shaft. "Rock yourself, slut. Show me how much you want this. Show me how much you want to please me."

I started rocking forward and back as the shaft slid easily in and out. The breadth of the rod filled me completely as each pass aroused me more and more. At times, I felt the extra nudge she gave it; other times, she'd pull back just as it was about to ram me. I rocked harder. I wanted to feel it spreading me wide as it moved. I craved being filled completely. It was *so* good that I didn't want it to ever stop.

"Easy, boy," she whispered, her voice much breathier than before. "Slow down. Make it last. We're nowhere near finished, are we?"

I blinked and tried to calm my ragged breathing. I knew what she wanted. It would be a long time before I'd have permission to come. I tried to slow, but the sliding shaft with its rippled edge rubbed against my clit on each pass. It made me buck harder and faster. Each time I rocked back, the feeling of the shaft ramming into me ignited my entire being with light after light. The stretching of my clit as it passed sent shock waves clear to my brain. Before long, I was lost in the sensations, going from motion to motion, my breath labored. Forward and back, forward and back, the rhythm pulsed through me like her music did. I was lost in the ecstasy of the feelings. Pumping back and forth, the instrument filled me with more than just sensations. Waves of pleasure washed over me, drowning me as my mind went blank, only physical senses entering my consciousness. I wanted to write poetry. I wanted to write songs of love and lust. I wanted to sing them out as my body was singing from the pleasures it was taking.

Then, just as I couldn't control it any longer, as I was going to come, she pulled back, taking the shaft out of my body. I gasped as the emptiness filled me, my muscles searching for the instrument that had been there.

"What, boy? Do you want more?" she asked as my body shook with frustration.

"Yes, please, Mistress." I panted, shaking my head from side to side as tiny quakes rocked me, telegraphing my need.

"My little slut needs more? Enough to beg?"

"Yes, please, Mistress, I beg of you," I said, about to lose my mind as I shook. "Please, give me more. I want to please you so much more."

Then she laughed, that cold sadistic laugh that chilled me. "No, not this time. Not yet. I think you need to learn who's in control."

I closed my eyes tightly, trying to keep my mind from trembling with fear that I'd done something terribly wrong.

"Please, Mistress, you're in control. I beg you…" Tears ran down my face.

"Not good enough, boy. Who's in control?"

I was frantic, wanting to complete the marvelous sensations, frenzied with trying to find a way to appease her. "You are, Mistress. You're in control."

"How much in control, boy?"

"Total control, Mistress." I wanted to scream, the pain of the tension between my legs becoming unbearable.

"Why do I have total control, boy?"

My mind raced, trying to find the right answer. If I could just think straight.

"Is it because I own you?" she prompted.

"Yes, Mistress, yes," I wailed. "You own me. I'm your boy. I'm yours totally."

"Then you'll do whatever I ask?"

"Yes, please, whatever you want, Mistress."

"What if I want to stop now?" Her voice was getting that cold aspect that scared me because I needed more.

"Yes, Mistress, whatever you wish." I was almost hysterical. I prayed it wouldn't be that. "I only want to please you, Mistress."

"Then are you sorry that you tried to pleasure yourself on the rope without my permission?"

"Oh yes, Mistress. I was bad. I beg your forgiveness." I was groveling, but my body still tensed. "Please forgive me, ma'am. I'll never try that again. I promise."

"A promise? Not without my permission?"

"Yes, Mistress, I promise. Never again." I was ready to pledge her anything, I was so tied in knots.

"Such an obedient, repentant, contrite boy." She stood as if to walk away. I lowered my head to the floor. Her footsteps paused. Was she trying to decide when I'd had enough? The minutes crawled by.

"If I were to continue...*if* I were...you wouldn't come without my permission, would you?"

"No, ma'am. Never."

"Never?"

"No, Mistress. Never."

She lurched forward, driving the shaft deep within me. I almost cried out. I was flying off but trying to keep what control I had. I gasped as she rammed me again and again. Finally, I heard, "Come to me, boy."

"Thank you, ma'am," I screamed as my body exploded into thousands of magnificent sensations.

CHAPTER SEVEN

I barely felt her helping me up from the floor where I'd lain in her arms for a long, long time. She sat me on the wide bench, saying "Stay right here." Then she was gone.

I let myself float in the magnificent aftermath of the deepest orgasm I'd ever experienced. I chuckled as I glanced at the long rubber dick discarded on the floor. Yes, Neisy had been right. Helen certainly was a master at its use. I lay back and drifted in and out of sleep for quite a while but finally had to get up to use the john. Helen was standing there as I came out.

"Didn't I tell you to stay on the bench?" she asked. "And what are you doing on your feet?"

I dropped to my knees. "Forgive me, Mistress. I had to go. And I was so overtaken by your magnificent training that all else fled my mind." I waited, head bowed. Would she buy that crap? It took all I could give to keep from laughing.

There was silence.

Then she broke out into her wonderful laughter. "You are so full of yourself, boy. I don't know whether to reward you or beat your butt raw. Crawl over here."

I crawled to her and bowed my head to the floor.

She paced, a habit I was getting used to but still found

intimidating. I waited to see where she would stop…in front of me or behind. She did neither but sat on the bench. I waited. "The next time I tell you to stay somewhere, you stay. If you have to go, you'll hold it until I say you can move. If you can't do that, I'll have to chain you down, and believe me, it'll be in a way you won't enjoy. Do you understand?" Her voice was low and threatening.

"Yes, ma'am."

"When I tell you to do something, do it immediately. If I tell you to stop, freeze right where you are. If I say hurry, you run, not saunter. Am I clear?"

I took a deep breath. "Perfectly, ma'am."

"Come over here."

I crawled to where she sat and waited.

"All right, boy," she said, "what have you learned?"

"That I have to be able to control myself," was my immediate answer.

"And?"

I thought. "And that I have to be patient for you to make the decisions for me. And that I must obey your wishes."

She leaned back. "That's a good start, boy. Now, do you like being whipped?"

"Only if it makes you happy to whip me, Mistress." I smiled, still looking at the floor. I knew that was the answer I should give, but I also realized it was absolutely true.

"And if it didn't make me happy?"

"Then I wouldn't like it."

"Why do you want to make me happy? Why put yourself through all that just for my pleasure?"

Where was she going with this? "Because you are my Mistress," I ventured, hoping that was what she wanted.

"But why do you allow me to be your mistress?"

"Allow you?" I asked, surprised.

"Yes. You had the choice. You're here of your own free will. You've chosen to stay. Why?"

"Because you asked me to." I was beginning to get flustered.

"No, I didn't ask you to. I asked you if you wanted to."

"I...I thought you wanted me to."

"Whether I did or not, why did you stay? You're not here for the money. With your talent, you could support yourself quite well. In fact, I'm paying you a good bit of money for your musical talent. Why are you here...in this situation? Why are you staying with someone who loves to torment you?"

I couldn't find an answer. At least not the answer I thought she wanted to hear. "Because I want to be yours," I decided.

"Come up here and lie on this bench."

Slowly, I crawled up beside her, then lay on the bench facedown, my head toward her. She began caressing my back, then my butt, carefully massaging the marks, some from the night before last that had started to fade, and four bright red ones from last night. I closed my eyes and melted into her touch.

"Do you love me?" Her voice was soft.

At first, I wasn't even sure I'd heard her correctly. "Yes, Mistress," I whispered. I was surprised she'd asked.

"Are you sure, boy?"

"Oh yes." Without hesitating, I turned, gazing up into her eyes. Our eyes met for a few seconds. Realizing what I'd done, I turned away quickly. "I'm sorry, Mistress. I didn't mean to do that. I'm sorry I raised my eyes to you. I beg your forgiveness."

Her hand on my shoulder was gentle. "That's all right, Little Butch. That time was forgiven."

We stayed there for several minutes with her stroking my back. Her gentle touch made the pain of the past twenty-four hours more than worthwhile. How was this happening to me? Was it really love and not just infatuation or idolatry?

At last she stood. "Either lie here on the bench, or if you want to, sleep under it. You still may not stand. And don't go anywhere else. I'll be back. Don't disappoint me."

❖

I lay there for quite a long while, trying to figure out what had just happened. Helen had been warm and gentle, the way I had always pictured her in my dreams, not the rigid, demanding mistress I was growing used to.

Soon, Neisy came with my lunch: a sardine sandwich and another glass of carrot juice. Not two of my favorite foods, but I ate them in silence.

"Don't forget to clean the dick and put it away," she reminded me as she took my empty dish and glass and left.

Ah, yes. First things first. Don't get all sentimental.

CHAPTER EIGHT

The afternoon dragged on. I was bored almost to tears. I wasn't used to only sitting around with nothing to do. I could hear her playing the piano downstairs. What I really wanted to do was to immerse myself in one of her tapes. I crawled under the bench and curled up for a nap. Neisy woke me with dinner, a piece of fish and a green salad with a vinaigrette dressing. And a cup of coffee.

"You must have done something good today." Neisy laughed as I ate in silence. "There was liver waiting for you and another glass of carrot juice!"

She waited, but I just smiled.

"You learn quickly. I expected a response."

My only response was a chuckle.

"Well, whatever it was, she's been in a good mood all afternoon. Better watch it, you never know what she's planning."

I gasped and stared with a questioning look.

"Don't ask me." She shrugged. "I just know her well enough. She's been smiling all afternoon, so she's got something up her sleeve." She looked up at the clock. "Six thirty," she said as she took my empty plate. "You won't have long to wait. Nine is usually her time. Better get ready. I'll let you enjoy your coffee. Just wash the mug and leave it in the bathroom. I'll get it later."

With that, she left.

Six thirty, I thought, another whole two and a half hours. What could I do to kill the time without going crazy from boredom? I took the chance and went into the bathroom with my coffee to run myself a bath. There was bubble bath on the shelf above the tub so I added some of that. Then I sank down into the warm, foamy water.

❖

The door opened at 8:30. It was Neisy. "Well, Little Butch, I still don't know what she's planning, but somehow, I'm a part of it. She gave me the order to come up here and get ready for 9:06. I hope you haven't gotten me in hot water."

I looked at her with my best "Who, me?" look.

"Yes, you," she said as she slipped out of her clothes and hung them on the hook behind the door in the bathroom. "I'm going to shower. Better hope your knees hold out."

I sat beside the bench, listening to her shower. Damn, was that the most exciting thing I could think of to do? Boredom had become the worst torture of this whole experience. I'd already cleaned the dungeon; inspected all of the equipment in the armoire, making sure they were all clean and neatly placed on their hooks and shelves; and I'd made sure that everything in the bathroom was tidy, in its place, and clean. What was it I'd read somewhere about a man in prison who mentally took his motorcycle apart and rebuilt it to keep from going crazy? Could I perform a whole Beethoven sonata from memory?

I'd just gotten to the bridge of the "Moonlight Sonata" when Neisy came out of the bathroom patting her still-damp hair, which she'd carefully combed back. "I don't know how you manage all that hair," she said. "It's beautiful and thick, but it's so long. It must take you hours every day just to get it dry. I don't think I've ever seen a butch with such long hair."

I ran my hand though the long mass that would have landed at the bottom of my collar if I'd been allowed to wear one. I'd thought of getting it cut short several times but had never gotten around to it. I'd had it short when I was in college but had let it grow since. Maybe now would be the time to get it cropped again. I'd have to ask Helen where there was a good hairdresser.

"It's almost time," Neisy said, pointing at the clock. 9:00. "She said to light the candles and wait." Neisy looked at me with an evil grin. "I hope she's planning what I think she's planning. You'll love it." She smiled and, humming to herself, began to light dozens of candles from the bottom of the armoire and set them around the room. Finally, with the light off so we were lit by candles, she turned back to me. "Better get ready just in case she's early. Assume the position."

We knelt in the center of the room, our backs to the door. It was barely a minute before we heard it open.

"Ah. My two little ones. Such a pretty sight," she said. "Neisy, once again, I'll need your assistance. Please stand up."

"Thank you, ma'am."

"There's one other thing I want you to do for me tonight. How good are you, boy?" Helen asked.

"Ma'am?"

"How good a lover are you?"

"Uh…well, I haven't had any complaints." I smiled.

Her laughter filled the room. "I guess we shall see. Neisy…stand in the middle of the room."

I glanced up. Helen took me by the arm, placing me directly in front of Neisy, still on my knees. "Do her, boy. Let me see how good you are."

Neisy and I froze. We looked at each other, unsure.

"Either you eat her out, or I'll do something you won't like half as much. What will it be? I'm sure neither of you will enjoy the way I'll do her."

The tone of Helen's voice sent chills through me. The warmth of the evening had completely gone. Unsure, I reached to touch Neisy's legs. Helen stood behind Neisy and spread her legs farther apart. Slowly, I leaned forward and kissed Neisy's thighs, slowly licking upward until I reached the soft, shaved triangle between her legs.

Helen pushed her against me. She felt foreign. I had never thought of her as a lover. She put her hands on my shoulders, guiding me as I nibbled the edges of her triangle.

"Make love to her as you would to me. Neisy is mine. Therefore, Neisy is me," Helen said.

With that thought, I didn't need more urging. My tongue sought the orb that lay hidden within the folds. I drew her into my mouth and began sucking as my fingers sought the source of the wetness. Neisy gasped as I thrust into her. Her breathing became ragged as her hips started to push against me.

"Is it good, Sweet One?" Helen asked.

"Oh, yes, Mistress. Very good."

"Tell me about it, sweetness."

"Oh, Mistress," Neisy murmured. "Strong hands, like yours...taking me..." Her voice trailed off into a deep sigh.

"That pleases me."

I didn't need more encouragement. I attacked my prize with renewed enthusiasm. I shot my tongue up into her crotch. Damn! Why wasn't my tongue longer? I slurped her wetness as I ground her clit between my lips, harder and harder. Soon, Neisy was grinding on my hand, my mouth, my entire face.

"Mistress, please," she whimpered, shaking. "I want to come."

"Right now?"

"Yes, please, Mistress."

"Not yet, sweetness. Let's see what the boy can do."

I continued my mission, sucking everything in. The heat in the room seemed to soar. I put the ache in my neck out of mind and continued licking and sucking, slowly but strongly, driving my fingers in and out of her wetness.

There was a long silence as Neisy's hips thrust. Without thinking, I slid my hand all the way into her cunt as if she'd sucked me into her. Only heavy breathing came from above. I felt her trembling on the brink.

"Yes. Come for me now," Helen said in a husky voice.

Neisy's hips bucked against me as she orgasmed against my mouth. Her muscles tightened around my fist as a low growl escaped her throat. As the tension eased, I slipped my hand out. Once again, Neisy shuddered in orgasm. We remained there as if frozen until Neisy started to calm.

I rubbed the back of my neck to get the stiffness out.

"Not bad, boy." Helen moved around me and leaned down to whisper in my ear. "Now, what turns you on? Where is your zone?"

I shook my head. I didn't know.

"I know you like your tits tortured. What else?" She reached down to grab my breasts. I gasped as my whole body reacted to the pain that raced through me. I heard her chuckle. "What else, boy? This?" She wrapped her hand around my throat the way she had before. I sank into her as my bones seemed to melt. "Yes, that's it, isn't it?" she whispered as she squeezed a little tighter.

My mind floated away. I didn't even know if I could or should breathe. The feel of her hand holding my throat sent me into a whole new dimension. The room, Neisy, everything faded into a mist.

"Oh, we'll have to explore this, won't we? This could be a whole new thing for you. We'll just have to experiment." As she released me, I realized how hard I was breathing. I fell forward onto my hands. I felt her rise and heard her talking to Neisy, but I couldn't have recounted what she said.

Finally, I realized she was standing in front of me. "You'll stay here. You know the rules. Do I have to repeat them?"

"No, ma'am."

"Be a good boy. I'll be back."

I sank onto the floor. What had just happened? Why had I reacted like that? Was this what she'd meant when she'd talked about zoning? I didn't have a clue. I crept the few feet to the bench and crawled under it. I was asleep almost immediately.

Chapter Nine

When I awoke, Neisy was gone, the candles had been extinguished. and the lights had been turned very low. I stretched to get the stiffness out and realized I needed the bathroom.

Of course, when I came back, Helen was standing there. How did she always know when I was doing something wrong? I sank to my knees.

Helen just stood there and shook her head, her foot tapping on the floor. A few moments of silence passed as she paced around me. "What can I do to make you follow rules, boy?" she asked. "Why is it so important to stand when you know I want you to kneel?"

It seemed rhetorical, so I didn't answer. She walked to the armoire and searched. I heard metal clinking...heavy, thick metal. I didn't dare look up to see what it was. Then she sidled to the platform against the far wall. "Kneel, up here."

I crawled onto the platform and rose onto my knees.

"Straighten your back. Tall." She wrapped a heavy, wide metal collar around my neck. It was so wide I couldn't lower my head. I felt as if I was in one of those cervical collars for sprained necks. It was so hard I couldn't move my head more than an inch right or left and nowhere up or down.

She locked a chain to the collar that led to a ring embedded in the wall. I had to stay upright. My knuckles could barely reach the floor.

"Stand up and turn around. You didn't want to crawl. Now you can't. Are you satisfied?"

"Mistress," I began, but a sharp slap across the face stopped me. I looked up and barely kept from shaking in fear.

She glared as I lowered my eyes. With my head held up by the collar, it was hard not to look at her. Finally, she smiled. "I was going to shackle you to the wall, but I think you need to learn self-discipline." She lowered the chain that hung from the ceiling to the right. "Hold this." She moved my hand up the chain until I was stretching fully. She did the same with the chain that hung to my left so I was stretched against the wall.

"If I handcuffed these to you, it would be easy. But it's not going to be easy, is it?" She stepped back. "If you don't hold the chains, they'll swing away, and it'll be quite a feat to retrieve them. So, you'll have to hold on tightly. And you wanted to stand, so now you have to." Her leer frightened me. Finally, she smiled. "I'm going to bed now, but if I come back in and you've dropped the chains, I could get very, very angry. You don't want to make me angry, do you, boy?"

"No, ma'am."

"No. I know you don't." She turned and walked away, turning the light off as she left.

I was beginning to like the pain and was getting used to dealing with the boredom. I could stand here in bondage and not hate it, but I could not handle the darkness. I took a deep breath. I hated the dark. I wasn't frightened; it made me angry. Being in the dark reminded me of when I was a child and I'd had the measles. My mom had darkened all the windows in my room and made me wear a blindfold until the fever and rashes disappeared, an old way of protecting a patient from eye damage.

And I had hated being sick. I could hear the other kids playing in the street, but I couldn't even get up to watch them. I just had to lie there.

The anger in me rose now. Hadn't I told Helen about being alone in the dark? Hadn't I listed it as one of my limits? I was pretty sure I had. Maybe I hadn't. If I had, then why had she done this?

I waited.

My stomach started to tighten. I thought I might throw up, and panic started to set in. What if I made a mess? What would Helen think? How long would I have to stand here with vomit all over me, the smell and the taste growing stronger minute by minute?

"Stop it!" I whispered to myself. "You don't have to throw up. Control. That's the answer. You can control yourself. That's what got you into this. That's what will get you out." I tried to control my breathing and leaned against the wall. Time passed. Or at least it felt like hours were creeping by.

"Breathe slowly," I told myself, "from the diaphragm. Like you've been taught in voice class. Slowly. In through the nose. Out through the mouth."

That's it. Controlled breathing. In. Out. In. Out.

Anger began to replace the panic again. I didn't have to be here. I could break the contract whenever I wanted. This kind of torture wasn't part of the agreement. But if I stopped now, would it mean I'd stop it forever? Would I have to leave? Would I never see Helen again? Never feel her touch, never have her smile at me?

Damn.

I contemplated dropping the chains. If I loosened my grip enough to kneel...but the chain to my collar wasn't long enough. I could barely touch my knuckles to the floor. I thought of yelling. Was I going crazy? I thought of dropping everything.

I didn't.

I cried.

❖

I couldn't think. There was just the tightening in my chest and in my stomach, the pounding in my head.

It could have been ten minutes or ten hours, but it seemed like an eternity. I could hear the clock ticking, but I couldn't concentrate to count the seconds. Was it the clock or my heartbeat? It seemed to speed and slow at random. I had no way of telling what was real and what wasn't. The room was pitch dark, not even a sliver of light under the door. I couldn't remember where anything was. The darkness blocked direction and distance. Something could have been inches away, and I'd never know it. I listened carefully, but all I heard was the click of the clock as second after second slid by.

The door swung open without warning, and the light from the hallway blinded me. I screwed my eyes shut. I couldn't see who was there, but I hoped it was Helen.

Please God, let it be Helen.

I waited, my heart pounding so violently, I couldn't hear if someone came into the room.

A voice whispered in my ear. "Have you stood long enough, Little Butch?"

"Yes, Mistress. I've learned. I'll never disobey you again. I promise. *I promise!*" The tears started to flow.

The cuff loosened around my neck, and as soon as it was

removed, I dropped the chains and fell to my knees, my head to the floor. Except for the clink of chains banging against the wall, there was silence.

"See, Neisy? It didn't take much time at all. Not even two hours."

Two hours? Two hours! I wanted to rub my eyes. The light still burned them, but I couldn't open them yet.

"Neisy, light some candles and shut the door. And get him a handkerchief for his nose."

I heard giggling as Neisy walked away. Soon, the light mellowed, and I could open my eyes. I felt a brush of air as a wad of tissue dropped beside me.

"Clean your face, boy. You look a little bedraggled."

I wiped my face and blew my nose. It took several tissues to get all the sweat, tears, and snot, especially from my position.

Neisy massaged my back. Soon, I began to regain my composure, and my breathing returned to normal.

"What did you learn, boy?" Helen asked.

"That I will obey whatever you say, ma'am."

"Did you enjoy that lesson?"

"No, ma'am."

"Will you disobey me again?"

"Oh no, ma'am."

Neisy leaned close to my ear. "Thank her for teaching you this."

"Thank you for this valuable lesson, ma'am. You're very generous to teach me."

Helen chuckled. "Is that what you were thinking while you were standing there?"

"No, ma'am."

"What were you thinking?"

"How messy it would be if I threw up," I blurted.

Helen let out a wonderful loud laugh. I smiled as I felt her displeasure flow away. Neisy seemed to relax, and her stroking became lighter. At Helen's command, she brought me a glass of water that I greedily gulped. I hadn't realized how dry I'd become. When I finished, I lowered my head to the floor.

"Well," Helen said, a smile in her voice. "I think there's one more lesson this boy has to learn tonight."

"One more, ma'am?" My God.

"Lie on the table."

Not knowing what to expect, I crawled to the low, padded table and lay on it.

"On your back, boy. You won't get out of it that easy."

I rolled over. Anxiety returned to my stomach.

Helen smiled and took leather straps and bands from the armoire. She handed some to Neisy to attach them to my wrists and ankles. Soon I was spread-eagled, held by the straps attached to the thick hooks. "Comfy, Little Butch?"

I licked my lips. "I…I guess so, ma'am."

Helen sat beside me and caressed my face. "We're going to reach a new zone tonight, my Little Butch, so I want you to be very careful. Do everything I say. And for this scene, I want you to look me in the eyes the whole time."

"Ma'am?" I asked and slowly looked. I was amazed by the intensity in her eyes. I felt as if I was falling into them, completely overwhelmed. A moment passed as I felt awash in her.

"That's very good, my sweet boy. I think that this will be your forte. Do you like candles?"

I glanced at the dozen or so candles of different sizes and heights. My eyes fell back into hers. "Y…yes, ma'am."

She held her hand out, and Neisy gave her a candlestick with a long white taper. Helen shielded the flame from the air as she moved the candle over me.

"Candles are so beautiful and shed such wonderful light,

don't you think?" she asked, smiling with a glint in her eye. "Candles can do such wonderful things."

As I stared into her eyes, the candle tilted to let a large drop of melted wax fall on my stomach. "Oh!" I cried as it burned.

Helen stared deeply into my eyes. "You'll like this, won't you, boy?" She smiled as she let another drop fall.

I writhed as the fire spread. Then I took a deep breath as my skin cooled the wax into a solid.

"Keep looking at me, boy. I want to see your eyes as you become part of this candle."

She seemed to blur as the drops fell; she worked her way upward in a thin path between my breasts. I tried to keep my eyes on her, but my focus kept following as she watched the wax.

One after another, the drops sent a searing fire that seemed to burn through my flesh into my heart. The candle came closer and closer, the wax becoming hotter and hotter. The burning was exquisite. I floated, reaching up to meet the wax. At some point, someone held my wrists as I writhed. The wax bored into me, scorching me in an exquisite pattern of light, pain, and pleasure.

A thin path of wax grew around my breast. I tried to watch, but I floated higher above the table as the flames floated above me. I wasn't on this planet. I didn't want to be. I wanted to fall into the candles, to become a part of them.

Cool hands stroked me. Where I wasn't sure. Someone spoke, but the ability to translate sounds had left me. I was awash in the flood of sensations. Someone lifted my head, and a cool substance lapped at my lips.

"Try to drink this, boy. Swallow it. Remember to swallow."

It took a minute to remember how, but then I was gulping water. I drank as if I hadn't had liquid in days.

A beautiful face floated above me. "Welcome back, Little Butch." Helen's soothing voice, a warm smile across her face.

"That was incredible, Mistress," I murmured, still miles away.

"Yes. Yes, it was."

Then I asked the unthinkable. "Is that all, ma'am?"

Helen broke out into a hearty laughter. "I think this little wax slut wants more." She glanced at Neisy. I couldn't take my eyes off her face.

"Give it to him, Mistress." Neisy's voice.

Helen turned back to me. "Do you want more, boy?"

"Oh yes, ma'am. Please."

"Can you take more without calling your safe word?"

"Yes, ma'am." That phrase was becoming a mantra that soothed me.

"What is your safe word?"

I had to stop to think. "Boston."

"Very good. Remember it. You may need it soon. Why do you want more wax?"

"I...I want to go there again."

"You like flying that much?"

I must have nodded because Helen laughed the evil laugh that sent shivers through me. This time it seemed like a song. "Are you sure?"

"Oh yes...I'm sure." At that point, I would have begged if I had to.

"Ma'am?" she asked.

At first, I wasn't sure what she wanted.

"Have you forgotten your manners, boy? You're asking for more and not even addressing me properly?"

I tried not to hyperventilate. What if she denied me? "I'm sorry, ma'am...Mistress. Please...if you'd like to, please. I can take some more, ma'am. If you want to give them to me."

There was that laugh again. "Then you shall have more." And the drops began again.

It was better than any of the drugs I'd tried in college. I flew higher and faster than I'd ever experienced, no matter how expensive the dope had been. I'm not sure how long it lasted or even when she stopped, but I caught her voice flowing out of the stratosphere.

"He really knows how to zone, doesn't he? I've never seen anyone go that far on the first try."

"Yes, ma'am. It was magnificent." Neisy stroked my face. "I don't think I've ever seen anyone take it like that."

"Well, Sweet One, you can zone that far, but it took you a while to reach that level." She lifted my head again. "Swallow more of this; your lips are dry."

I gulped the cool liquid.

"Do you know who you are?"

It seemed like such a silly question, but I had to search for the answer. "Mickey? Your Little Butch?"

Helen laughed again, warmly this time. "That's very good. I wasn't sure you'd remember. There's just one more step, Little Butch. We have to get this off you now."

She chuckled as I looked down at my body. I was covered with a thick layer of wax. Most of the candles had burned down to nubs. Only two still burned, and the lights were on.

"This will be the fun part. I want you to watch carefully." She held a hunting knife, ten inches long. I took as deep a breath as I dared.

Helen grinned. "Do knives scare you?"

"Yes, ma'am." I could barely whisper. All of the flying I'd done a moment ago had abandoned me and left me in a deep, dark hole that was threatening to bury me in tons of ash.

"Then you'll have to be very still." She smiled as she began to scrape the wax off my stomach with the blade.

Barely allowing myself to breathe, I watched as she cleaned the wax from my body. The blade cut through the wax as if it was butter. I didn't even want to speculate on what it could do to my skin. As she worked her way toward my breasts, I held my breath.

"I'd breathe if I were you, Little Butch. Just hold very still." With that, she flicked a large glob of wax from my left breast. I inhaled sharply as it flew away.

"Your nipples will be the fun part." Helen smirked. "Maybe I should just cut those nipples off so they'll be nice and smooth. That way we wouldn't have to worry about the wax."

I whimpered. Did I really need to get the wax off? Maybe it would melt off if I took a hot shower.

"What do you think, Neisy?"

I heard a giggle behind me. "The Mistress is just playing with you."

"Are you sure?" Helen asked. I gasped as a chunk of wax fell from around my nipple. I was, gasping. I was about to lose it. I'd never been afraid of knives before. It seemed so absurd.

I giggled. I could feel all my emotions just below the wax, fighting to get out, but there were so many; I couldn't control them. I laughed hysterically. Tears flowed from my eyes, and a deep sob overwhelmed me. I had to laugh at the thought of it, too. Laughing and crying at the same time but I didn't know how to stop. I was on a carousel spinning out of control, faster and faster.

Helen stroking my face calmed me. "Shh, Little Butch, It's all right. Shh," she crooned. "I have you. You're safe." She moved closer and murmured to Neisy to release my wrists. Then she held me, rocking me as I laughed and cried into her shoulder, clinging to her.

"Please, Mistress, should I use my safe word? I don't think I can take knives tonight."

There was a long pause. "No, my Little Butch. I'll be very careful. Close your eyes, and it'll all be over in a minute."

I slammed my eyes shut. "Thank you, Mistress."

I could still feel the blade. Finally, she removed a patch that had fallen between my thighs. "That's all of it, boy. You can relax and breathe." Helen drew me into her arms again. I sobbed in relief. "This has been a roller coaster for you, hasn't it?"

"Oh yes, ma'am," I said as I buried my face against her breasts. Compared to the knife, her body felt so safe and warm.

"Did you really think I would cut you?"

"No, ma'am. But I was so afraid of the knife. I've never been afraid of them like that before."

"You zoned to new heights tonight. That can leave you feeling vulnerable. I should have foreseen that."

As Neisy unstrapped my ankles, I curled up against Helen, who held me close and rocked me until my breathing had calmed. "Next time, ma'am. I'll try harder next time."

"You tried very hard this time, didn't you?"

I nodded against her.

"Such a good boy," she whispered. "When you're ready, shower, get some clothes on, and come on downstairs for breakfast. I think you need a really good meal."

❖

I was still dazed when I went downstairs, but the food Neisy put in front of me looked so good, I couldn't push it away: poached eggs on toast and cold orange juice. I didn't realize until I finished that both Helen and Neisy were staring at me.

"Pretty hungry, weren't you?" Helen chuckled.

"Yes, ma'am. I've never tasted anything that delicious."

"You can get very hungry when you travel that far."

I nodded with a shy grin.

"Maybe we'll have to keep him out of the dungeon, or our food bill will be astronomical."

I bowed my head in apology.

"Either that or let him starve," Neisy suggested.

I looked at her with fear in my eyes.

"Now, she's kidding," Helen said. "I won't mind if you eat me out of house and home if you continue to please me like that."

I grinned. "Thank you, Mistress...for everything."

Helen sat back with a wide smile on her face. "I feel you've completed the training I had for you, boy."

"Already?" I was amazed.

"You learn fast. Can I count on you to control yourself?"

"Yes, Mistress."

"What do you think, Neisy?"

Neisy looked at me in thought. "Aside from learning how to set a table, I don't think there's much more...for now."

"And what do you think?" she asked me.

"Whatever you wish, Mistress," I said without hesitation.

Helen smiled at Neisy. "Well, there you go. Come over here, boy."

"Yes, ma'am," I said and sank to my knees beside her.

Helen took a box that had been sitting on the table. "You'll wear this to signify that I own you. Not when you leave the apartment or when others come to visit. Do you understand?"

"Yes, ma'am." I smiled nervously. This was turning into a major moment.

"You still want to belong to me, don't you?"

"Yes, ma'am, I do."

She buckled a brown dog collar around my neck. "Remember all you've learned in the past three days. Don't be too conceited about this, and be aware that you represent me in everything you do. Do you understand that?"

"Yes, Mistress." I glanced over at Neisy with her delicate black collar, and she smiled at me.

"What was the most important thing you learned, boy?"

I didn't hesitate. "To control myself, ma'am."

Helen looked proudly at Neisy. "You officially have a brother, Sweet One. Treat him well." Then Helen looked back at me. "Training is complete…for now. Have a cup of coffee. You have a lot of work to do. The music's been sitting there for days!"

Chapter Ten

My life grew to revolve around Helen; not that it hadn't before, but now I had a purpose, a goal. I transcribed her music at the piano, and I pleased her in the dungeon. No matter what she wanted, I jumped to every command. I lived in heaven, and I melted whenever she said, "You please me, boy."

The days grew into weeks before I realized it. I got Helen's permission to call Frank and sort of explained what was going on. I told him I had more work than I'd thought, and I wouldn't be back in Boston for a while, but that everything was going well. He suggested he go to Ann's and put my belongings in storage. I said no, that I didn't know how long I'd be in New York or if it'd be permanent but that I'd keep in touch and was having a wonderful time.

Helen was sometimes home during the day, other times not. She spent a lot of time in the recording studio or in rehearsals. The first recording was always as she wanted it. She never needed a second take unless someone else made a mistake.

Evenings at the apartment had fallen into two categories: Easy, when Helen would sit in her chair and read or go over the day's manuscripts while Neisy and I watched TV or listened to music and read. And hard, when Helen wanted us in the dungeon. Sometimes, she'd want both of us; other times, just one.

I began to look forward to the dungeon. Something inside me had snapped that night with the wax, and I looked forward to everything that happened there. I'd always enjoyed sex. With men or women, it had been a favorite pastime, but over the past few weeks, it had become almost as important to me as my music. Not vanilla sex, where everything was gentle and loving, and I ended up feeling as if I needed to get married. Heavens no. I wanted the pain and floating, the rough sex that I kept giving and giving until there was nothing left...then I started again. The pain was becoming exquisite, and I was amazed at how much I could take. The more my body hurt the next day, the happier I was.

❖

One night, Neisy put the radio on in the middle of the living room and swayed to the music. As it got faster and wilder, so did she. Soon she was grinding, her hands moving over her body, eyes on Helen. I sat there on the floor, mesmerized. As Helen stroked my hair, I realized that Neisy's seductive movements were having an incredible effect. Helen watched with her eyes slightly closed, an evil grin beginning on her face.

"Little Butch," she whispered. "Why don't you dance with Sweet One. She looks so lonely dancing by herself."

I got to my feet and let the music flow through me. Soon, I was dancing close to Neisy, our bodies touching, veering away, touching again. Neisy put a hand on my hip and guided my pelvis to hers. We rubbed and crushed, our eyes locked, and the music melted us together. Our breasts mashed against each other. Our eyes were only for each other and for Helen. We danced closer and closer, each move becoming more seductive. Each look to Helen became more suggestive. The rhythm was like a drug, and soon we were both in it.

Then the music stopped.

Helen stood at the radio, her eyes half-lidded. "Let's take this upstairs."

Neisy had a satisfied smile spread across her face. "Come on, boy," she said, grabbing my hand and pulling me up.

We barely made it into the dungeon before Neisy was stripping. Neither of us was allowed to wear underwear. Naked, she grabbed me, pulling my shirt over my head.

Before we could get on our knees, Helen was in the room. "Continue."

I didn't know what had gotten into us, but within seconds, I was rolling on the floor with her, my cunt wet and throbbing. I pushed Neisy onto her back and covered her with my body, kneading into her flesh, gulping her.

The sex was, hot and hard. Neisy's wetness covered my face and hands. We couldn't get enough of each other. I explored every inch of her with tongue and fingers. Her fingers dove into me.

She moved to accept my entire hand. As my fist balled within her, her writhing became frenzied, her hips bucking against me. Moans of "Yes! Oh yes!" escaped her lips. She reached to bring me closer and without thinking, I moved over her. If my arm could have bent the other way, I would have placed my cunt directly over her face. As it was, we sixty-nined each other with her hand on my ass and her fingers delving within me.

Helen encouraged us as we moved. Her voice was as hot and breathless as mine would have been if I wasn't so busy biting, sucking, and lapping. I pushed back against Neisy's hand, which felt smaller than Helen's. I was hot, and I wanted it. Her fist slipped neatly into me.

I flexed and turned my fist in her, mirroring the movements. It felt as if I was fisting myself. If I twisted a little to the right, the hand in me twisted to the right. I'd push in deeply and be pushed into deeply. Both of us breathed in gasps.

"Please, Mistress," Neisy said. "Please, I have to come."

"Just a minute," "Helen whispered. "Boy, are you ready to come?"

"Oh, yes, ma'am. Right away. Please!"

"No, not yet."

Helen's command drove me crazy. It felt as if we were going to swallow each other. After a few minutes, she said, "Together. Come to me."

Both of us pushed into each other, our bodies covered with sweat and sex. I felt as if I'd never stop coming. When we withdrew, we both collapsed, gasping for air and sated.

Helen stood over us, a strange look on her face. "Beautiful," she breathed. "I've never seen that before. You two are very creative. And very hot." Then she turned and left. As Neisy moved to curl up in my arms, the door closed.

Chapter Eleven

More days went by. The pile of tapes diminished as the pile of music grew. The opera was almost transcribed. Now I just had to orchestrate it. I went blithely from day to day, waiting for Helen's commands and working on the music. I couldn't have been happier.

Neisy, however, became very sullen. I found myself being careful around her, as it was easier to step out of her way than risk a slap on the rear or a snide remark. She had me confused. There were times when she went out of her way to be nice. Other times, I felt like dirt scraped off her shoes. She assigned me the most menial jobs around the apartment. She seemed above all that now.

Helen left on Tuesday for Atlanta: some rehearsals, a concert, some partying. She'd be back Monday night. We'd been told to behave ourselves while she was gone and not to annoy the neighbors. As she left, she gave each of us a warm embrace and a kiss on the forehead. When Saturday came, Neisy seemed even more disagreeable, sending me to the corner store four different times. She could have given me a list to begin with.

I was arranging parts for the brass ensemble that would accompany the opera. Before she'd left, Helen and I had sat for several days, going over her ideas for the orchestration. I could hear in my mind exactly what she wanted. It would be a piece of cake I wanted to have done when she returned.

Neisy leaned against the door of the piano room, watching me. "You really are the ultimate bottom, aren't you?"

I looked at her, surprised by her tone. "What do you mean?"

"You know what I mean. 'Oh, Mistress, this is wonderful. Oh, Mistress, that would sound great. Oh, Mistress, your ideas are spectacular.' Little brownnose, worming your way into her ego. Don't think I don't notice."

I sat still, surprised by her tirade.

"It gets tiresome, you know. All she ever says is 'Little Butch did this,' and 'my boy said that.' She hardly ever speaks to me except to sing your praises." A hateful look crossed her face. "You're trying to get me out of here. I can see through your sham."

"Don't be silly, Neisy. She'd never get rid of you. You're the number one bottom here. That hasn't changed. She gives you more in the dungeon than she gives me."

"That's because she doesn't want to harm her precious little boy." Her ire could have filled the room.

I shook my head, wanting this to be over. She walked over and grabbed the music.

"Neisy!" Before I could get it back, she ripped it in pieces, crumpling them into a tight wad. The ink, still wet, smeared across the paper. I stared. "Are you crazy?" I stood there shaking. Two days of work lay in a ball on the floor. Maybe I could piece them back together and copy them, but it would take time.

Neisy grabbed me by the shirt collar. "Get upstairs." She sneered, giving me a shove.

"Upstairs?" I was shocked.

"You do remember where the dungeon is, don't you, little boy?"

Anger raged through me. "Helen said we're not supposed to go in there without her."

"She also said you sub to me. Or have you forgotten that part? You say I'm number one? Well, prove it. Get upstairs." She took a step closer, and I could smell alcohol on her breath.

"You've been drinking."

Before I could react, Neisy backhanded me across the face. Her slap held quite a bit of power. I stumbled, stunned. I touched my face to soften the pain and felt the warm wetness of blood. Her ring had cut my cheek.

"What the hell is wrong with you?" I yelled. "Are you crazy?"

"Not anymore." Her voice was low with anger. "I was crazy to let Helen bring you in here."

I put up my hands to ward off the new blows she leveled at me. I didn't want to hit back. She was stronger than me, but I had to stop her. I took several steps backward to get out of her reach.

She sneered again. "You can't get away. I'll beat the shit out of you."

"Wait. Just wait," I said, trying to think of something to calm her. "Let's talk about this, okay?"

"I'm tired of talking." She took another step.

I sprang and pushed back with all my strength. As she fell, I raced for the door and flew out of the apartment. I heard the door slam behind me as I took the stairs three at a time, down four floors to the street.

❖

I walked around the Upper West Side for hours and sat in the park overlooking the river until the light started to fade. Then I got up and walked again. It was dark before I got back to the apartment building. Will, the evening doorman, was on duty, so it had to be after eight.

"Nice night for a walk." He smiled as I came in, but then his face turned shocked. "My God, what happened to you? Were you mugged? Are you all right?" He put his arms out to comfort me and sat me down in the chair behind his post.

I hadn't realized how disheveled I must have looked. As he took out his handkerchief to daub my cheek, I realized there was still blood from Neisy's attack.

"Let me call the police," he said, reaching for his phone. "Where did this happen?"

"No. Don't call the police. Please." All I could think was the mess we'd be in if Helen found out what had happened or if the police got involved. "It was an accident. I'm okay. I just tripped."

He frowned, clearly not believing a word I said.

"No, really," I assured him, trying to keep my voice calm. "It was just a stupid accident." I took a deep breath. "Do you know if Neisy's home?"

"She went out about a half hour ago."

At least I could go upstairs and clean up without facing her.

"I don't know where she went, but I could call someone else in the building if you need help." His voice showed real concern.

"No." I sighed. "I'm all right. I just need to lie down."

"Are you sure there's not something I can do?"

"No. Thank you, Will. I'll call if there's anything I need."

"I'm here till two. Then Robert comes on duty," Will said after me. "Call if you need me."

"I'll do that. Thanks."

At the apartment door, I had a panic attack. Did I have my keys, or had I rushed out without them? I dug into my pockets and finally extracted the key to the door. I sighed in relief. At least I wouldn't have to wait in the hall for Neisy to return.

As I walked to my room, I caught a glance at myself in the hall mirror. No wonder Will had been so concerned. Both sides of my face were bruised a light but noticeable black and blue. The cut to the right of my upper lip was oozing. I looked as if I'd been run over by a truck.

With a sigh, I went into the bathroom and started the water for a warm bath. As an afterthought, I added several spoons of Epsom salts. I figured if they soothed my body after an evening in the dungeon, they might help now. As I stripped and lowered myself into the tub, a thought struck me. How could I explain the bruises to Helen? I didn't want to get Neisy in trouble but, hell, she'd started it. Anger filled me as the water rose around me. But then, so did concern.

❖

Neisy didn't come back to the apartment until late the next morning. I heard the door open and close and her footsteps in the hall. I was in the kitchen making coffee when she walked in. She stopped but lowered her eyes and walked by without a word.

For the rest of the day, we both tried to stay away from each other, it seemed. Neither of us spoke, and I could taste the tension in the apartment. Neisy stayed in her room most of the day, the door closed. She only came out to use the bathroom or refill her coffee cup.

Around seven, I filled a second bowl with the black bean soup I'd made and walked to Neisy's door. I knocked.

"What?"

I opened the door. She was lying on her bed, staring at the ceiling. "I thought you might be hungry," I said, placing the bowl on the table next to her bed.

"Hmph."

I waited a minute, then turned to go.

"What are you going to tell Helen?"

I stopped. I hadn't expected her to talk to me. "I don't know."

She looked away. "Me, either."

I waited, but she showed no other sign of talking, so I closed the door behind me.

❖

I watched Helen get out of the cab from the music room window. The doorman took her bags from the driver and paid as Helen rushed into the building, looking happy to be home.

"She's here," I stated as I turned toward the living room where Neisy lounged on the couch. We hadn't talked since I'd brought her the soup. I didn't know what to say, and I was afraid of saying something that might make her angry again. I wasn't sure why she hadn't spoken, but I hadn't asked.

Neisy rose at the sound of Helen's key in the lock and went to take the suitcases from the doorman. She kissed Helen on the cheek as she threw her coat on the couch.

Helen patted Neisy's cheek and started to say something but stopped when she saw the gloomy look on Neisy's face. "What's wrong, Sweet One? Aren't you glad to see me?"

Neisy glanced at me as I stood in the music room door. Helen followed her gaze and stopped. "My God. What happened to you?" She rushed over and hugged me.

I'd tried to mask the bruises on my face with makeup, but

I knew she'd see through it. At least the swelling in my cheek had gone down.

She held me at arm's length and examined my face. I averted my eyes, not wanting to see her when I lied to her. "It's nothing. I fell."

I prayed she'd believe me, but of course, she didn't. I glanced at Neisy, and Helen turned to her. "All right," she said, her teeth clenched, her voice in that low tone that meant she was not pleased. "Which one of you is going to tell me what happened?"

"It's nothing," I started to say as Neisy began speaking. We stopped and looked away from each other, embarrassed.

Helen studied us both, then turned to Neisy. "Upstairs. Now."

Neisy ran up the stairs, not looking at Helen or me.

Helen took my face in her hand. I winced as she touched a bruise on my cheek. "I'll talk to you later. Wait here."

"Yes, ma'am," I murmured as Helen followed Neisy upstairs.

I paced the living room for a full hour before I heard my name. I hurried upstairs, knowing Helen was angry and that every minute she had to wait would make her even more so.

As I entered the dungeon, I spotted Neisy sitting, fully clothed, in the center of the floor. I'd half expected to find her bound and whipped, but the look on her face told me it was far more serious than that.

"Now give me your side," Helen said. "And no bullshit about falling. I want the truth."

I shrugged and stared at the floor.

Helen waited, her fingers tapping impatiently against her thigh.

"We fought."

"Who started it?"

Please, don't make me say this. I stared at the floor in silence and shrugged.

Helen turned to Neisy. "Do you have something to say to her?" That stopped me. Helen had referred to me in the feminine. Was I no longer her boy? That was the worst blow of all. It seemed everything was falling apart.

Neisy still wouldn't look at me. "I'm sorry I hit you," she said in a soft voice.

"I can't hear you," Helen roared. "How the hell can you expect her to?"

Neisy finally looked up. "I'm sorry I hit you. I was drunk. I took out my frustrations on you. I apologize."

Helen turned for my reaction.

I shrugged again. "Okay," was all I could say.

"Okay? Okay? She tries to beat the shit out of you, and all you can say is okay? What is wrong with both of you?" Helen stomped to the other end of the room, then turned and slowly paced back. "I must have trained you too well," she said, looking at me and shaking her head. She sat on her stool and held her head in her hands. "I go away for not even a week, and I have to come home to this?" She sighed, then looked us both squarely in the eyes. "Clear this up between you, and I don't want to see either of you outside this room until it's settled. Either kiss and make up or kill each other. The choice is yours." She strode out.

I shifted back and forth for several minutes. Neisy picked imaginary lint from the rug. The tension grew. Finally, Neisy exploded. "All right," she yelled. "I'm sorry! What else do you want me to say?"

I sank onto the floor. "I don't want you to say anything," I cried in frustration. "I just want this to be over. I want it the way it used to be."

Neisy shook her head.

"What did I do? What made you so angry at me?"

She looked at me for the first time. "You didn't do anything. You were perfect." I started to object, but she stopped me. "No, it's true. You do everything she asks. You never fail. You never make a mistake. You can do her music, and you make her happy in here. You're perfect. What's left for me to do?"

"Oh, Neisy, I'm sorry."

"Don't be. This was coming on for a long time…long before you got here. It was just a matter of time. I can't give her what she needs. She feeds off you; she gets her musical ideas from you; she gets her thrills from you. Whether you know it or not, you challenge her. She has to be creative to top you. That's what excites her. I'm old meat." She took a deep breath. "I've asked her to release me."

"Neisy, no—"

"She needs you. She's never needed me. I was just a nice diversion, and I'm a good cook. I never challenged her the way you do, no matter how hard I tried."

"But you love her." There had to be something I could do to stop this.

"That isn't enough. Not for Helen Robins. She thrives off someone who makes her be creative. That's you, not me. It never was me." There was a sadness dripping from her voice.

"I'm sorry."

"Me, too."

I hugged her, and her arms encircled me at last. We rocked back and forth, trying to comfort each other. It felt so final.

Chapter Twelve

It was lonely not having Neisy around. Although she called now and then from her new home with her new master, it wasn't the same as having a friend to share things with. Helen hired a woman, Rachel, to come in during the afternoons to vacuum the downstairs, change the bedding in her room, and cook dinner. I still ran all the errands and purchased the food from the list. And I kept the dungeon spotless. I also continued working on the music.

In the extra time, I started working on my own music. Copying for Helen had ignited my own creative spark, and I was starting to compose music of which I was proud. In fact, working through Helen's music was making my own playing better. Helen had even commented that I sounded smoother and more relaxed in my delivery. I glowed in her praise. And I grew in her light.

Occasionally, she'd play old tapes for me...old scratchy tapes recorded years ago on recorders of low quality, when she'd been on the road as part of a band that toured the "chitlin' circuit," going from town to town playing one-night stands in townhalls or speakeasies, making just enough money to keep food in their mouths and shoes on their feet. The sounds from those tapes filled me with wonder. There was exquisite joy in the dances and such misery in the blues. I could almost see the laughter and tears they'd felt as they played. I'd never in my life thought I'd be so totally immersed in the music.

In those days she'd managed to keep her sanity from the racism that flowed through the country, both north and south, and avoided the drugs that flowed in the back rooms, in alleys, and on buses. It had been a hard time for musicians like her. Her eyes bored into me one day, and she warned me to stay away from drugs.

I knew my eyes betrayed me.

"Have you tried drugs?" she asked.

"In college. But nothing hard. Just pot."

"Stay away from that, too. It's sneaky. It'll catch you just as hard as the others, and you'll never know it."

"Yes, ma'am."

And there were times she introduced me to recordings of other jazz musicians, some of whom were her friends. I grew to know the music of Dizzy Gillespie, Charlie Parker, Thelonious Monk, Marian McPartland, and many others. My musical education was growing.

And my sexual life was changing. It was as if my whole world had been turned inside out. Things I'd thought I'd never do were now things I longed for. There were days that my back was so sore I couldn't sit against the couch. I couldn't sleep on my stomach because my breasts hurt so much. And I was in heaven. Anything Helen wanted to do, I'd gladly accept.

I had really fallen hard. My whole being was wrapped in her. I knew she loved me, even though she never said it. I saw it in her eyes and felt it in her touch. She brought me little presents, a teddy bear that had a leather collar or a keychain with a black leather buckle that snapped over my belt; small things, but things that said she'd been thinking of me.

We spent our evenings either listening to music or

watching TV or in hot sessions upstairs. I was learning to make my mistress happy and more than not, our sessions ended with, "You please me, boy."

My pain tolerance had soared higher than I ever thought it would. I welcomed the feelings. Usually, I wanted more. My mind didn't flinch from new sensations. And there were some I even dreamed of, some I asked for, others I could only hope were on Helen's list. She never repeated anything, always adding some new twist that would startle me, make me stop in fear. I never knew what to expect. And that was what excited me most. I was in love with the challenge, pushing myself past new limits.

Not all the sessions were filled with pain. Some were on how to stand, where to sit, how to serve Helen and her guests, what was expected of me in every situation within this new community, anything that would bring honor to my mistress.

Other sessions were filled with a type of psychological fear that was like living in a horror movie, the kind where I couldn't take my eyes off the screen even though my heart was running at a thousand beats a minute. Helen knew where all my buttons were and what type of threat would make me sweat. Yet I always ended up wanting to scream, "Scare me again! Scare me again!" And so Helen played with my fears, making me go down into the bug-filled storage rooms in the basement to look for something or blindfolding me during a scene and making me think there were spiders walking over me. She played with knives until my curiosity overcame my fear, and I begged her to shave the wax off me with a straight razor. The look on her face as she scraped the wax made it all worthwhile, even though I almost passed out from holding my breath.

The days Helen was away on tour stretched so very long. I'd work on her music; I'd work on mine. I'd listen to the radio or read. I'd wander around the neighborhood. And I'd sleep. Hours seemed to creep by. I did everything I could think of to fill up the time, waiting to see her taxi pull up out front and get the call from the doorman. And once Helen was home, there were wonderful nights upstairs.

One night, I stood, legs spread, hands on the horse, leaning forward and trying not to fall as Helen's flogger splayed its tails across my back. Flogging had become a favorite warm-up for both of us, usually leading to stronger things. Once warmed, I was ready for anything, and Helen was usually more than willing to take whatever she wanted from me. I gave it all without hesitation.

This time, I fell into the cadence of Helen's strokes, lulled by the rhythm. I almost didn't feel the fall of the leather against my skin. The pulse of the flogger spoke to something deeper inside me. Suddenly, I started to giggle.

Helen's strokes stopped. "You find this funny?"

"No, ma'am," I answered, trying to stifle my laughter but not doing a very good job of it. "I'm sorry."

"What's going through that crazed mind of yours?"

"You skipped a measure," I answered, not doing well at stopping the laughter that seemed to ooze out of my every pore.

"I...skipped a measure? Of what?"

"Miles Davis. It felt like you were playing one of his songs." There was silence, and I grew afraid that I'd said just the wrong thing.

Helen burst into laughter. With relief, I joined her, and for a few minutes, we were both overwhelmed. Helen's dissolved into the deep coughing that I'd heard quite a bit lately. I felt her step away and heard her sipping the glass of water that was always within reach.

"Davis..." she whispered, stepping back to me. "Just wait

till I play some Coltrane on you." And with that, she started flogging me harder and faster, the thuds becoming stings. The strikes became overwhelmingly swift. One upon another upon another until there was no division between them.

I was sinking into that space far outside of consciousness, soaring into that nothing zone, not even aware of Helen or the room or if I was standing or sitting or floating. Time and space ceased to exist.

Then I was in Helen's arms. She held me tightly to her soft breasts. I sank against her, letting my head fall against her shoulder. How long she'd held me, I couldn't begin to measure. When I was able to stand, she moved away with the warning, "Don't move. I've got something for you."

I waited as I heard her searching the armoire. As I felt something around my waist, I looked down. She was fitting a dildo harness around me, a hard-on bigger than I'd ever imagined.

"Uh…"

"Be my big boy tonight," she whispered. "You can do that for me, can't you?" One hand on my ass, she stroked the dildo sensuously with her other. "Such a good strong dick," she said, moving the shaft so that the base rubbed my clit. "You know how to use it, don't you? It's time my little boy grew up and learned to please his ma'am."

I waited as she caressed my ass and the dick. At first, I didn't know what to do. The hard shaft extending from my crotch looked so foreign. But as Helen continued, I felt the movement of her hand through its length as if it really was me. As I closed my eyes, I felt it becoming a part of me. I wanted to be her boy more than anything else.

"Come on, my Little Butch." Her voice was soft and smoky, deep with passion. Still wrapped in her arms, I went to the padded bench, which had been spread with a thick quilt. I couldn't tell if I was dreaming; my mind was still somewhere in outer space. She laid me down on the bench and reached to kick off her shoes and remove her panties. She left on her skirt and the sleeveless shell that covered her wonderful breasts.

I wanted to say something, but I couldn't form the words. I knew this was something wondrous. I wanted to make Helen happy no matter what it took, no matter how long. Was I really going to make love to Helen Robins? Or was I hallucinating something from my zone state? It seemed so unbelievable, as if I'd suddenly walked into another dimension. Would I wake up under the bench?

Helen stretched her body along mine. She caressed my breasts, down my stomach, and onto the staff above my mound. I moaned as her teeth sank into my neck. Not knowing what I was doing, I reached for her, grasping her shoulder. Her soft skin against my fingers felt hot and moist with perspiration.

She whispered as she moved over me. "Service me well."

She lowered onto the shaft, steadying herself with her hands on my shoulders. Slowly, she eased up and then back down. As she moved above me, the base of the shaft beat against my clit, and soon, I was pushing up into her, both of us in rhythm, our breathing becoming ragged. Helen flew harder and faster. I worked to keep up, marveling at her passion and stamina. She pumped up and down as I thrust into her until we were both writhing harder and harder. I heard her moans but was too engulfed in all the sensations. I couldn't control it anymore. I moaned loudly as I came, my body driving into her.

Her breath stopped as her body stiffened. I felt her wetness oozing over me and her body grinding down onto me.

"Oh, my boy, so good. So very good," she said as she lowered herself onto the bench and pulled me on top of her.

As she stroked my face, she whispered, "You do please me so very much, Little Butch, you really do."

I leaned into her, holding her close. Those were the words I wanted to hear. Yes, that was my mission in life.

The next morning, I awoke under the bench, a place which had become as comforting as the bed downstairs. I folded the quilt and the harness and started to clean the dildo. I still felt Helen's warmth and power radiating from it. I brought it close to my nose, smelling her sweetness. Closing my eyes, I brought it to my tongue and tasted her. Last night roared through my mind again, and weakness attacked my legs, making it difficult to keep my balance. The taste of the stiff shaft was Helen. It was wonderful.

I laughed. The absurdness of what I was doing raced through my mind. Was I really standing here getting high sucking my own dick? Was that as outrageous as it seemed at that moment? What was happening to me?

I cleaned and oiled the harness and dildo, a smile on my face. Life was very good.

❖

As I sat at the piano, I couldn't help but stare while she sat at her desk, editing my work or rewriting her own. Her beauty glowed. I could see what most people never saw. There were days when she looked older, when gray hair peeked through, and the lines hadn't been hidden by creams and makeup. But the beauty in her heart radiated through her smile and her eyes. When she read something she liked, joy lit up her face brighter than any light bulb. Those were the moments I lived for.

There were mornings when she sat and coughed a smoky

hack which she drowned with glass after glass of carrot and celery juice. Yet she still lit up inch after inch of Shermans. She'd leave them to burn out in the glass ashtray, relighting them when she rose out of her concentration. There were times when she played piano with a cigarette wedged between the middle and ring fingers of her left hand. I laughed because she seemed to forget it was there, playing long after it burned out. I'd collect half cigarettes from every ashtray in the apartment, some only lit and left.

We joked about it from time to time, but I'd learned not to push her about anything. She did what pleased her. The blasted carrot juice, which I'd grown to hate the taste of, was open for teasing as long as she was in the mood. When she was tired, I held my tongue, trying to not be Mickey Mouth. I'd learned when and if I could joke around.

But when I watched her play, everything seemed to melt away. She glowed, and the years faded from her face. Her smile became animated, and her eyes were like a child's. Her sound kept getting brighter and brighter; the speed of her fingers, faster and faster. But then, it may have just been me.

I fell deeper in love with her. I lived from one night to the next, waiting for the touch upon my neck or the whip upon my back. I wanted to hear "8:13" or "7:53," hoping it would lead to, "You please me, boy." She'd been prophetic when she'd said, "You will feel pain because it pleases me to give you pain. And you will be grateful that I have allowed you to please me." I craved her pain, and I was so very grateful that I belonged to her, that she allowed me into her life. Boston, the Arts Center, Andrew, and Ann faded into a past when I didn't belong to Helen.

Chapter Thirteen

One afternoon, I came downstairs from cleaning the dungeon to find a man sitting and talking to Helen. He was a large white man, not fat, with a well-trimmed beard. He wore black jeans and a starched shirt with a beautiful black leather vest. He emanated an aura of power I'd never experienced. Helen seemed in awe of him, acting with a deference I'd never seen before. He sat in her black leather chair while she sat on the couch. I'd never known her to do that. I'd never seen anyone sit in that chair but Helen. It seemed forbidden.

"Is that him?" he asked in a bass voice.

I didn't hear Helen's answer or the conversation that followed, but soon Helen called me from the kitchen.

"Yes, ma'am?" I was unsure how to act. Was this a casual friend or someone from the lifestyle? Helen never called me boy in front of anyone. She snapped and pointed to the floor the same way she did in the dungeon when she wanted me to kneel. I sank to my knees, hands clasped behind my back, not knowing where to look. I chose the floor just to be safe. There was silence as I stared at Helen's shoes.

"He seems very trainable," the man said.

"He's been very good for me."

The man stood and paced the way Helen did in the dungeon. "Yes, I think I could work with this one."

My stomach rolled. Was Helen trading me? I glanced at her out of the corner of my eye, but she was watching him.

"Thank you, Master Lawrence," Helen said as she stood. "I'll have him to you next Wednesday."

"I have to go now, but stay in touch so we can finalize the details," he said. Helen moved to give him a hug. "And you be good for your mistress, boy." He patted my head and left.

I looked up, panicked.

"Don't be so scared, Little Butch," she said as she sank onto the black chair. "That was Lawrence, one of the masters in the lifestyle."

"Are you trading me?" I couldn't keep my fear from rushing out.

She smiled as she reached for a cigarette. I dove for the lighter and held it for her. She leaned back in her chair and let out a cloud of smoke. "No, boy. I'd never trade you unless you requested it." Her eyes were warm and loving. "But there are some things you need to know that I can't teach you. When I'm away on tour next week, you'll go and live with Lawrence and his family and learn some of the protocols of this life."

"I'll go live with him?" I asked, still fearful and sinking to the floor, sitting cross-legged.

"Just while I'm away. But it's time you earned your leathers. You should have more than that collar, but I'm not sure when to give it to you. Lawrence will decide if you learn your lessons well."

"Will he…" *How do I ask this?* "Will I have to let him…"

Helen laughed. "Only if you're a very good boy!" She chuckled. "No, Master Lawrence—and you will call him master or sir—and his top boy will teach you how to serve better and tell you more about the lifestyle." She ran her hand down my face. "I'm still your mistress, the one who's in control. You'll just observe and learn from him."

"But...will I have to be naked?" I felt all right with that with Helen, even in front of Neisy, but with others, strangers, around?

"Yes, while you're in training. But all the others will be, too."

"Others?"

Helen chuckled. "Yes," she said, running her hand along my cheek. "Master Lawrence has several slaves in his family, just like when Neisy was here. There's a pecking order within each family. Just like Neisy was my first, although you were first boy. You will learn the etiquette for dealing with each one."

I must have still had a panicked look on my face.

"There's so much to learn," she continued. "And if you want to continue, maybe even have your own submissive someday, you have to know the rules. You've been very good for me, but if we were to go out into the leather community, there are things that would be expected of you. I want you to know it all. Does that scare you?"

I took a deep breath. "Will I be there long?"

"No, but I'll be away on tour, a week or so at a time, for the next few months. You'll be with Lawrence whenever I'm away. Are you okay with that?"

"If it's what you want, and you think I need it," was my answer as I swallowed to relieve the dry feeling in my mouth.

"Just think of this as going to grad school." Helen smiled. "And this will be the classical course. I know how much you like the classics!"

❖

When Helen left to play her concerts and club dates, I went to stay in the Village with Master Lawrence and his family. Besides Robert, who was First Boy, the most important of Master Lawrence's submissives, there were two other boys and two girls.

When I arrived, a young woman opened the door and introduced herself as Julie. As she closed the door behind me, she took off her simple cotton robe and hung it on the hook beside the door so she was naked. "You have to take off your clothes," she said "Master doesn't allow any in the house."

I sighed loudly. "What if someone comes to the door?"

"That's what this robe is for. If you're allowed to answer the door, you'll put this on. You get used to it. Everyone here's naked except Master and Robert." She smiled. "I hear you're owned by Mistress Helen."

Owned? Yes, I guess I was. I knew she owned my heart and the rest of me by extension. "Yes," I said as I pulled my shirt up over my head. "Do you know her?"

"I've seen her," she said as she helped me fold my clothes. "But I haven't been allowed to talk with her. I've only been here five months."

"Five months?"

"Yes. Slaves aren't allowed to talk to anyone outside the house until they prove their worth. I hope I get approved soon. I'd love to call my friend Pam. She's gotta be wondering how I am." She waited while I picked up my pile of clothes, then led the way though the hallway and up a flight of stairs. We stopped at a room on the third floor. "This is where the girls stay. You'll share it with me and Sharon." She pointed to one of three mats on the floor. "You can have that one." Other than the mats and three footlockers, there was nothing else in the room, including a door. Even the door to the adjoining bathroom had been removed.

"Well, this place certainly won't get a four-star rating," I joked.

Julie chuckled. "Oh, Master makes sure we have everything we need. Put your stuff down. Robert's waiting."

I placed my clothes in the locker and followed her downstairs. Robert waited for us in an office. He sat behind a large desk that made him look small, but when he stood, I was amazed at his height. He must have been six foot four or five.

He dismissed Julie and turned to me. "You're Helen's boy."

"Yes, sir."

After a moment's consideration he said, "Sir is the Master. I'm just Robert. I don't think you'll get us confused."

"No, sir...er...Robert."

He laughed. "Well, I guess you'd better sit down." There wasn't a chair. That made Robert laugh even harder. "On the floor. Trainees aren't allowed furniture. Didn't your mistress tell you that?"

"I must have missed that." I sighed as I sank to the floor.

"Well, what else did you miss?" he said, sitting back down. He pulled out a folder and wrote my name across the top. "I see you're not shaved. Doesn't your mistress want that?"

Shaved? I hadn't shaved my legs in months. I must have looked bewildered because Robert wrote a few things into the file.

"We'll take care of that," he said looking back at the folder. "Mistress Helen says you're a masochist?"

I thought for a moment, then nodded. "I guess I am. There are times I crave the pain."

Robert nodded and smiled. "Sounds like it." He started a long list of questions about what I had or hadn't been taught. By the end of the afternoon, I was drained, but I didn't have time to stop. I observed how dinner was served that night. I'd have to start serving tomorrow. Only Master Lawrence and

Robert ate dinner at the table. The rest of us had to wait until the table was cleared, and Master had retired for the night.

As I was drying the dishes, I got a summons to report to the dungeon downstairs. I was to bring one of the girls. I raised my eyebrows at Julie.

"I'll go," Sharon offered. "It'll be nice to get my hands out of dishwater."

So off we went, not knowing what to expect.

"Lie here," Robert said, indicating a table.

"Did I do something wrong?" I asked.

He laughed. "No, my dear, not yet. But we have to take care of that hair on your body."

My hand went to my crotch. He laid a dish of soap and what looked to me like a very large razor on the table next to the bench. "Never been shaved before?" he asked as he pointed to the medical table.

I hoisted myself onto the padded platform. "No. Mistress never mentioned it."

"Well, I guess some women like their boys furry, but it will not do around here."

I sighed and laid back. What would Helen say when I came back shorn? Well, I'd find out.

"This looks like quite a job. But I think we can get it taken care of tonight," he said as he handed the soap to Sharon. "No hair except on your head. Understand?"

"Yes, sir," I whispered. "Er…yes, Robert."

"Don't go moving around, or one of us might get unlucky." He handed Sharon a second razor and began to lather me.

It took a good hour to get me shaved: armpits, legs, and pubis. Then I had a nice soapy bath. Sharon was with me for every move. I guessed she knew what a traumatic night this was. She hugged me and helped me dry off, and we washed and put Robert's equipment back in its case.

"Was that as terrible as you thought it'd be?" she asked when he left.

"No, I guess not," I answered. "But…what happens when it starts to grow back?"

She laughed. "You'll have to keep it shaved, or you won't be able to sit still it'll itch so much."

"Every day?"

"You'll get used to it. It'll be like brushing your teeth."

I was glad she was so confident. I sure wasn't. When I got back upstairs, I fell on my mat and didn't wake until the girls shook me in the morning.

❖

During my time there, I was lowest in status and took instruction from everyone, although Robert told me we were all equal. Except him. He had the same aura Lawrence did, and I had very little interaction with the Master. Robert took my training in hand. When he wasn't showing me something or explaining some aspect of the lifestyle, I had little time to myself. I served at the meals and was on hand if Master Lawrence or Robert needed something.

The others were friendly and warm, welcoming me like a member of the family. I could escape into a special safe room where the girls and boys could relax between sessions or when I had a time out. There wasn't any furniture, but it didn't seem necessary. At least we weren't afraid we'd bump into Master or Robert when we went about the house on an errand.

I witnessed many things that made Helen's dungeon seem like kindergarten, making me glad I was Helen's and not Lawrence's, but some things intrigued me, and I made mental notes to ask Helen. Lawrence and Robert were much more sadistic, and the sessions the other boys and girls had to bear seemed much more intense than I could tolerate, but then, I never knew until I tried. I would never imagine surviving some of those tortures when I was living in Boston.

The one thing that made my heart pump faster was when I witnessed Master Lawrence's fire play. Carl, Master Lawrence's third boy, was chained to the wall, already prepared for the session. I watched sweat run down his body as Master stepped up in front of him. He drew designs on Carl's chest with alcohol. Before the designs dried, he lit them on fire. In the dim light, the flames were bright as they ate through the designs. One quick flash, and they were gone.

Carl's eyes rolled back, and I saw him slipping into that zone where pain and terror didn't matter. As it continued, I could see how turned-on he was getting. Part of me wanted to be him. As the flames ate through the alcohol, Carl's masochistic desires were being devoured, too. The flame didn't linger and didn't burn, but the scene was so hot, I'd have to ask Helen to flame me, and I'd light up the city.

On the day I'd return to Helen's, Robert called me into the office. "What have you learned this week?" he asked as I sank to my knees.

I had to think about it. "Where to stand in reference to mistresses and masters. How to pour wine. And if anyone has a formal dinner, I know where to put all the forks and spoons."

He nodded. "Did you enjoy your week?"

"Most of it."

"You'll have more of a chance next week. I gather you'll be with us for another several lessons. Your mistress arrives home at five today. Hurry home and get ready. You want to be clean and fresh. I'll see you next week."

"Certainly, Robert."

I learned so much in the short times I was there: a myriad of ways to serve my mistress well. From then on, I didn't always enjoy staying at Master Lawrence's house. I had to spend most of the time on my knees, and they began to look bruised, and I was only allowed to join the other subs in the safe room twice a day.

I'd gotten over any embarrassment about my nakedness, though, and I enjoyed the look on Helen's face when I showed off my knowledge. She seemed impressed when I set the perfect table for her dinner. And I enjoyed the look in her eyes when I first appeared shorn. She demanded a full inspection and seemed happy I was dealing with it so well, making her proud, and that pleased my heart most of all.

CHAPTER FOURTEEN

As I answered the phone one day, a very husky voice asked for Helen. I recognized it, but the name, the face, escaped me. "May I tell her who's calling?"

Then came the laugh I'd heard a hundred times on her recordings. "It's Roz."

Of course, Rozalyn Maxwell, one of the greatest jazz vocalists in decades. I turned to Helen, who sat at her desk going over some of the manuscript. I mouthed, "Roz."

"Oh, wonderful," she said, holding out her hand for the phone. "Sir Roz! How was your tour?" Helen's voice fell into the sexy timbre she only used upstairs.

Helen and Rozalyn? Friends, yes. But more? As Helen caressed the phone, I realized I was jealous. Helen kept her voice low, whispering in a sultry manner. I went into the kitchen to get a cup of coffee. When I returned, Helen was hanging up the phone.

Her eyes lingered on the receiver, then up at me, a strange look on her face. "Roz is coming over tonight...for a drink," she said, accepting the glass of carrot-celery juice. She sat back pensively as she took a sip. "I haven't seen her in months."

I waited; this was obviously going to be an intimate reunion. "Should I...be out?"

Helen looked at me thoughtfully, then shook her head.

"Oh no. You'll enjoy her." I couldn't make out the look in her eyes, but I had a feeling that enjoy was not the word she wanted to use. I started to go back to work.

"Hold on a minute." She sat forward. "Let's talk. Sit down."

I sat on the floor, sipping my coffee.

"Roz is…well, you know that's Rozalyn Maxwell."

"I recognized the voice."

Helen smiled. "Well, Roz is an old friend. We go back a long way. I want you to know how to behave when she's here. You don't want to offend her."

"Why would I offend her?"

Helen paused. "Roz is a very…uh, special person. In public, she's a marvelous singer and one of the premier divas in the world." She took a breath. She had an odd smile that I couldn't translate. "However, in private, among her friends, she's known as Master Roz, a title she takes very seriously. She's much butcher, more masculine, in private than you'll ever see on stage. Refer to her only as sir. Don't make the mistake of calling her ma'am; she detests that. Do you understand?"

"Definitely." I took a deep breath.

Helen sat back and reached for one of her Shermans. I took the lighter from the table and held the flame out to her. "Tonight, dear Little Butch," she said with a grin, "you must be the most attentive, doting little submissive in the world. It's important to me. Roz will be so jealous."

"Jealous?"

"Roz and I have had a long-running feud over who has had the best submissive." She winked. "You're definitely in the running, so tonight is mine." She sat back, taking a long drag and smiling.

"Is there anything special you want me to do?" I wasn't sure where this was going.

She thought for a moment. "Yes." She looked at her watch. "Go and shower. Then meet me upstairs. I've something I want you to wear." She picked up the manuscript and made some quick notes as I left.

Freshly washed and naked, I waited in the dungeon. Helen entered a few minutes later. She had a white bag under her arm. "I was going to wait to give you this when Lawrence said you've earned it. He thinks you're pretty close, but I think tonight's a much better time." She opened the bag and took out a pile of black leather. "I hope these fit." She handed me a pair of soft, black leather shorts. I looked around for underwear. "No underwear," she ordered.

Not believing my eyes, I stepped into the pants and zipped them up. They fit like a soft, buttery glove. The leather hugged my hips, leaving my midriff bear, then stretched tightly across my stomach and ass.

"Perfect. Now this." It was a short black vest. It, too, fit me perfectly, coming just below my breasts. "Turn." I turned slowly, modeling the outfit. She studied me. Then she looked deeply into my eyes. "Are you devoted to me?"

"Of course. How can you ask?" I felt afraid. "Haven't I pleased you?"

Helen ran a hand through my hair. I leaned into her touch, eyes closed, waiting. "You've pleased me a great deal. I just wanted to be sure." She reached into the bottom of the bag. "Kneel."

I sank to my knees, feeling the leather around my ass object to bending but aware that this was something special.

She unbuckled the collar I always wore. "You already know most of your trappings, but I want you to be aware of the significance of what I'm giving you now. The old pieces of leather you've been wearing were just beginners' leathers. It's time you wore leathers that showed what you've learned. The old collar is just a token, a training collar, a constant reminder of your place here. This collar, a black leather collar, signifies that you've been trained as my boy, that you've learned how to be mine. I don't collar my submissives lightly. This is a form of commitment. It says I'll protect you, and you'll serve me. Do you agree to that?"

I nodded. She held the collar out.

"Kiss this and thank it for making you mine," she whispered.

I ran my lips over the smooth surface. As I kissed each inch of the collar, caressing it, tears welled in my eyes. I mumbled my thanks, both to the collar and to the heavens.

She placed the black collar around my neck and buckled it, making sure it was tight but loose enough not to restrict my breathing. She held out a small gold lock. "I have seldom locked a collar. Even Neisy wasn't locked, although she'd sworn to be my slave, but I want you to know how seriously I consider our relationship as Mistress-owned." She inserted it into the buckle of my collar. "You belong to me now. Is that what you wish?"

"Yes, I belong to you. I've always belonged to you." My heart felt like it was swelling many times its size. Yes, I belonged to her. I was owned. I was complete.

I was used to feeling a collar, but this was different. The stiff, cool leather was a new feeling, not uncomfortable. It would be a constant reminder of my devotion to Helen.

She took my hand and led me to the mirror. "What do you think?"

The look shocked me. I'd never seen myself in such a skimpy outfit before, except at the beach. Black leather and flesh. My arms and shoulders bare, as well as my midriff. And then the black strip of leather around my neck and the small gold lock. As I turned to view myself, I spotted part of a red welt across my rear.

"It's…incredible," was all I could utter.

Helen fingered the collar. "You'll only take this off to bathe. Or if we have company where it's inappropriate or if we have to go outside."

I stared at myself. I belonged to Helen Robins. I'd just devoted my life to her. Tears escaped my eyes.

She hugged me from behind. "You're beautiful," she whispered as she placed a light kiss on my neck.

The moment stretched.

"Now," she said, breaking the mood, "You need to know how to fix a drink for Roz. And I have to get ready." She squeezed my shoulders and led me downstairs.

❖

The phone rang at 9:00, Will the doorman. "Miss Maxwell is on her way up."

My stomach was doing jumping jacks. I straightened my leather and adjusted the collar as the doorbell rang. When opening the door, I bowed as Robert had instructed. "Welcome, sir," I murmured, knowing better than to look her in the face.

She handed me her coat and fedora, then strode into the living room as I closed the door. I hung her coat in the hall closet and set her hat on the table.

I could see leather trousers and heavy black shoes as she passed. They stopped, then turned. She grasped my chin and tilted my head up. I averted my eyes as she turned my face from side to side as if I was livestock for sale. I almost expected her to check my teeth.

Her touch was rougher than Helen's. "So, you're Helen's

new boy, eh?" She laughed. "Not bad. A lot better than the last one." She focused on my collar. I showed it off proudly.

"He's not for sale." Helen's voice boomed from the staircase as she made her grand entrance. She was dressed in the blue silk dressing gown that shimmered in the light.

Roz waited at the foot of the stairs as she descended. Helen held her hands out; Roz took them and placed kisses in both palms.

"Always the gentleman." Helen smiled as she drew Roz into a warm embrace. "It is so good to see you." She led her to the couch.

As instructed, I opened the bar and poured two shots of Kentucky bourbon over ice, then a single shot of vodka over ice and added a little tonic water and a twist of lemon. I offered the bourbon to Roz.

"Ladies first, boy," she said.

"I'm sorry, sir," I murmured.

Apologetically, I offered the vodka to Helen. "I beg your forgiveness, ma'am." Helen took her glass and nodded before Roz took her drink from the tray. Then I sank down on the floor next to Helen's feet as they continued their conversation.

I breathed a sigh of relief as they ignored me and started talking about Roz's tour of Japan and Hong Kong. Surreptitiously, I tried to observe. Roz was nothing like I'd expected. Her close-cropped hair was the same as the pictures on her albums, heavy doses of gray through the black, short and neatly slicked back. But her attire was different. Heavy black men's shoes replaced the gold pumps she wore in concert, and the black leather blazer over a starched white shirt was nothing like the beads and sequins of her stage persona. Master Roz was the complete opposite of Diva Rozalyn. As she sat back, her foot crossed lazily across her knee, she still exuded the regality I expected. I was having a hard time reconciling this butch dyke with the queen of jazz who floored audiences wherever she went.

I watched Helen, aware of each gesture, ready to grab the lighter when she reached for a Sherman. As Roz finished her drink, I jumped to my feet, took the glass, and refilled it. Helen refused a second refill. As they talked, Helen seemed softer, flirting, a side of her I hadn't seen before. It was a little confusing.

Roz's voice boomed into my consciousness. "So. Where'd you find this one?"

"Boston." She stroked my hair.

Roz laughed. "I didn't know there were any of those in Boston. The town must be beginning to loosen up. They still got those damn blue laws there, boy?"

"Some of them, sir. You can buy alcohol after 10:00 a.m. on Sunday now, and most of the stores can open."

"Worse than the South. At least in the South you can buy a drink any time on Sunday." She roared with laughter. I could tell that the second drink had relaxed her. "And collared, too. He must be special."

"Yes, very special." Helen ran the back of a hand down my face. "And a good musician. He's transcribing my music." I warmed as I felt the pride in her voice. I hoped she wasn't just showing off for Roz's benefit.

"Really?" Roz seemed impressed. "You're writing down all the notes that this madwoman plays?"

"Yes, sir," I answered, still surprised she'd spoken directly to me.

"You must have ears of steel." She laughed and turned to Helen. "Have you finished your opera?"

"Almost. I'm rewriting parts now."

"Anything in there I can sing? Something that'll make me famous?"

They both laughed. I was beginning to relax.

"Sure, baby," Helen cooed. "Come take a look."

I scrambled out of the way as they rose and went to the music room. Soon they were busy with the pages as Helen explained each section. I cleaned up the empty glasses and straightened the bar.

As I came back, Roz began to sing from the opera. I leaned against the door and listened. I was in heaven. They went through three or four of the pieces. I'd never heard anything like that before. It was spectacular, as if this was a private concert for me. Roz's voice soared as if the song had been written just for her and she'd been singing it for years. I wanted it to go on and on.

When it ended, Roz tossed the music on the piano. "This is incredible, woman!" She pulled Helen into her arms and kissed her passionately. As Helen's arms wrapped around her, I turned away. Waves of jealousy poured through me. How dared she kiss Helen like that? Helen refused to be kissed! *I should be the one to kiss Helen Robins.* I was the one who wore her collar. I fingered it, filled with doubt that it was real. Had Helen given it to me just to entice Roz?

I walked to the bar, trying to busy myself by straightening bottles and glasses as they talked. I felt Helen's presence behind me, then her hand on my ass. "Go upstairs and wait," she ordered in a husky voice. "Leave the collar on."

I looked at her, bewildered, then glanced at Roz, who watched from the doorway, a strange leer on her face.

"Make me proud," Helen whispered as a sharp rap on my rear sent me scurrying up the stairs. Roz's deep laughter followed me.

❖

Once inside the room, I began shaking. *Make me proud*? Was the warmth I'd heard for me or for Roz? What was going to happen?

I slipped out of the pants and vest and folded them. Then I waited, kneeling in the center of the room, back straight as Helen had instructed, my back to the door. The wait stretched on and seemed like hours.

Then the door opened. "Head on the floor, boy." It was Roz's command.

I lowered my head to the floor, aware of my naked ass high in the air. I heard her pacing. Then she hunkered down beside me. I didn't dare move. "Your mistress says you're very good."

"Thank you, sir."

"Do you think you're good?"

"I try, sir."

Roz laughed. "What can you do, boy?"

"Sir?" I asked, not sure what the question was.

"What can you do? What can you take? Your mistress says you're quite the masochist."

"If it pleases my mistress, sir."

"Does your mistress fist you?"

It seemed so personal, but I didn't dare not answer. "Yes, sir."

"With those monster hands of hers? And I see she whips you." She traced the marks on my backside.

I shivered from her touch. "Yes, sir."

"Quite a lot, by the looks of it."

"Yes, sir."

"Do you enjoy it?"

"If it pleases my mistress, sir."

Roz laughed loudly as she patted my rear and stood. "Spoken like a good little boy."

"Are you intimidating my boy?" Helen said from the doorway. As Roz hurried away, I used the moment to adjust my arms, support my head, and keep my forehead from rubbing on the carpet.

I felt Helen in front of me. She wore short black boots with thin heels and pointed toes. Oh, shit, this would be a heavy scene.

"On your feet." Her voice was strict but soft at the same time.

As I got up, she slipped her fingers inside my collar and pulled me to the horse. She tossed me over it, and I grabbed the handles on the other side. She stretched my feet apart and buckled on the separator bar. I tried to prepare myself for my pain zone.

But waiting was the worst. It seemed like days that Helen and Roz discussed the whips and lashes in the armoire. I finally heard them coming back. The first lash of the whip surprised me, and I cried out. There'd been no warm-up. It couldn't have been Helen. Then I remembered my manners. "Thank you, sir."

The response was another lash, but I controlled myself. It was harder than Helen usually started. The next ones brought tears to my eyes, but I refused to cry out or even whimper, though this lashing was much more intense. My ass burned. The thought that it must be bright red made me smile. I'd endure this. *Go ahead, Roz, do your worst.* I'd make my mistress proud.

The pain was building, the strokes so uneven that I jumped each time one landed. The wait between grew more excruciating than the lash itself, some so close together that the pain of the second piled on top of the first. How long could I last? I zoned into my bottom space. I wrapped myself in the pain like a warm fluffy comforter. Or was it the pleasure? It was more intense than any I'd felt before. I was under the lash of a master. I felt a surge of euphoria as I crossed that threshold. Just sensations. Not good. Not bad. Just marvelous sensations that made my body react the way my mistress demanded. I felt pride and exhilaration. I felt nothing.

Then it stopped. I was still waiting for the lash and jumped as Helen touched my neck. "Easy, Little Butch. You're doing so well," she whispered close to my ear. She stood in front of me, caressing my head as the tears fell. Her breathing was ragged, excited by the scene.

"Thank you, Mistress," I gasped, trying to catch my breath, but each intake of air only increasing the burning in my ass. I panted as the pain grew and grew. I pushed my head into her hands, hoping I could somehow forget the throbbing.

Then I felt Roz's hand on my cunt. "He takes fisting well?" I could hear the excitement in her voice.

"Oh, yes, very well, very deep." Helen stepped closer as Roz leaned against me. I heard them kissing as Roz grabbed my ass with both hands. Then Helen stepped back, and Roz's fingers drove deep into me.

"So very hot and wet. I almost don't need the lube," Roz said, her voice husky. Her fingers pushed in and out. I tried to concentrate on Helen grasping my collar. Anything to keep my mind away from the brutal invasion of my cunt. But my body was reacting, wagging back and forth in response to Roz' thrusts. I leaned onto Helen's hand to assure myself of that connection. I reminded myself I was doing this for her.

"You like this, don't you, boy?" Roz asked as she thrust deeper.

I was silent, trying to concentrate, trying not to gasp in pain.

"Don't you, boy?" Roz yelled as she thrust four fingers deep.

"Yes, sir," I cried as she pushed her entire hand into me.

I gasped and couldn't keep a wail from escaping. Her hand seemed twice the size of Helen's. It felt as if she'd reached up inside me and was squeezing my heart. I could feel her hand twisting and turning.

"Easy, easy," Helen said as she held my head.

Roz rammed me harder and harder. My body was about to explode. "Please, Mistress," I cried, wanting this to end. The pain and pleasure were almost beyond my endurance. "Let me come."

"Not yet." It was Roz's command.

Then the pounding stopped. But only momentarily as her fingers rimmed my asshole. I started to shake as she pushed a finger into me, her other hand still inside my cunt.

"Can he take this?" she asked.

Helen bent to look into my face. Tears and sweat covered my face, my nose was running, and I felt drool dripping from my chin. My breath was ragged and shallow.

Helen looked into my eyes. I wanted to beg her to stop this, but the encouragement that stared back made me say, "Yes." I would endure this because Helen wanted me to. I wanted to make Helen proud. I could do anything for Helen.

Then it began anew. As the hand in my cunt pushed, the finger withdrew from my ass. As it thrust in with a second digit beside it, the fist pulled back. I felt as if I was being scrubbed on a washboard, being opened like a ripe melon. My safe word popped into my head, but I bit down on my tongue as Helen caressed my neck.

My body began to quake. It was going to explode. I was going to come. There was no way I could stop it. I'd never felt this much pain...or this much pleasure. I was gasping. There was nothing but the inside of my body and the hands. So many hands. Hands in my cunt, hands up my ass, hands on my neck, hands on my face and on my back.

Then there was the screaming. Who was screaming? Was it me?

Suddenly, there was a scream, a deep wail. *"Boston!"* Who had yelled my safe word? Had it been me? Had I failed? All I saw was blackness. All I felt was pain. But the pounding stopped. Slowly, I felt the hands withdraw.

Someone was prying my hands from the horse's handles as arms pulled me back and laid me on the floor. Realization hit. It had been me. I'd yelled my safe word. I'd bailed out. I'd failed. I started to sob. Helen pulled me into her arms as I lay on the carpet, unable to move.

"I'm sorry," I sobbed. "I'm sorry I failed you."

That I'd failed her in front of her friend hit me harder than Roz's pounding. The one thing she'd asked was that I make her proud, and I hadn't been able to give her that.

"Mistress," I sobbed, devastated, "Forgive me. I'm sorry I failed you."

"Shh." She cooed as she rocked me, holding me tightly, caressing my face. How could she be so nice when I'd disgraced her?

"I'm sorry," I wailed. "I tried. Really, I did. I'm sorry. Forgive me, please."

She rocked me in her arms until I drifted into unconsciousness.

❖

It was still dark when I awoke. I was lying on the wide padded bench, a pillow under my head and a blanket wrapped around me.

Helen stood over me with an odd look on her face. She was dressed in the tight leotard top and leather skirt she'd had on the first time I'd seen her in this room; the same as she'd worn with Roz earlier.

"Mistress, I'm sorry—"

Helen placed her hand on my mouth. "You have nothing to be sorry for. You made me very happy. I have a reward for you."

"But…" Hadn't I yelled my safe word? Hadn't I disgraced her in front of Sir Roz?

Helen threw back the blanket and straddled the bench and my body. Slowly, she lifted her skirt. I gaped in astonishment. She wore no underwear! Black curls glistening with moisture floated just above my face.

"You made me very proud tonight. This is your reward." Slowly, she lowered herself onto my face. The smell, then the taste, overpowered me. Such a wonderful aroma, an incredibly delicious, salty, sweet taste. Greedily, I lapped the liquid, sucking it in, licking inside to get more. I savored each drop, amazed that I was so blessed.

Then I drew the hard clit into my mouth and caressed it with my tongue, relishing stroking the hard orb. I took it between my teeth and attacked it with my tongue.

Helen started to rock, at first lightly, then building as she pushed against me. I grasped her hips, steadying her. It didn't matter if I couldn't breathe; I was making love to my mistress. I had her gift in my mouth, and I was treasuring each moment. My wonderful stone mistress was allowing me to pleasure her. I didn't know what I'd done to deserve this, but I wasn't going to question it.

I worked every trick I knew, trying hard to pleasure her. At last I felt her body begin to quiver. I gave one last sucking flick of her clit as she pressed into my face, and I felt her shudder as she came, oozing across my face.

I gasped for air as she rose and pulled back. Sinking to the floor beside the bench, I realized that she, too, was gasping. "Mistress—"

"Shh." She stroked my face, a gentle, satisfied smile on hers. The moments hung together as our breathing quieted. Finally, she patted my face and said, "We can talk tomorrow. Sleep now."

She pushed to her feet and sat on the bench, drawing me into her lap. I clung to her, feeling the luxurious warmth radiating from her as I drifted back to sleep.

CHAPTER FIFTEEN

When I awoke, the apartment was quiet. Rachel wouldn't be in until afternoon, and I assumed Helen wasn't up yet. I rummaged in the kitchen, making coffee, toasting bread, looking for something, but not knowing what I wanted. I was sorer than usual but hadn't looked in the mirror to assess the damage. I'd do that once I had some caffeine in my system.

Carrying my coffee, I went back to my room. The face in vanity mirror was swollen and ashy. I looked like a truck had run over me. It had. A truck named Roz Maxwell. Definitely a diesel. I chuckled to myself. Then I saw the note on the bed. Clipped to it was a fifty-dollar bill.

"Little Butch," it read, "I'll be in the recording studio until at least five. Here's some cash. Treat yourself to a movie or some shopping. No work today. Promise? I'll be home for dinner. Mistress."

No work today? She didn't have to ask twice. I smiled as I went into the bathroom. As I let my robe fall, I turned to see my ass in the mirror. Bright red gashes crisscrossed my buttocks and the tops of my thighs. I admired the pattern they made, each welt evenly spaced and parallel, the marks of a master.

Taking the tube of balm, I smoothed it across my rear. It

turned pink as it mixed with the dried blood along the welts. I hadn't realized just how deep Roz's whipping had been. I examined them more closely using a hand mirror and realized that the skin had been broken in four or five places, and that there was heavy swelling beneath several other lash marks where the skin hadn't ruptured, but the blood had collected just beneath the skin. It amazed me that I was walking at all. No wonder it had hurt so much to sit up. I chuckled. This made my night with Stephen shrivel to a walk in the park by comparison.

I turned the faucets, checking the water to make sure it was not too hot. Then I went back into the kitchen and got a tray of ice. Taking a towel, I folded it into an ice pack and held it against my backside as I waited for the tub to fill.

❖

The day was a wonderful vacation. I went first to the Village and walked along West Fourth Street, looking at all of the windows, not yet wanting to spend the fifty dollars. West of Seventh Avenue, there were many other shops that advertised sex toys. I smiled to myself. How many of them had I already felt?

And to think how embarrassed I'd been to just look at them when I'd first moved here.

I walked slowly, every move causing my clothes to rub against the gashes on my ass, every step a reminder of last night. I was still confused by Helen's reward, but my smile widened each time I thought of it.

Then I stopped at one of the coffee houses off Washington Square and ordered a café au lait as a treat. As I sat there, pain still gnawing at my backside, I tried to decide how to spend my money. The thought of walking over to the Pink PussyCat and buying Helen a present crossed my mind, but I couldn't think of anything that didn't already hang in her armoire. I decided to walk a few more blocks before making my decision. As I passed one of the jazz clubs, I stopped to read the billboard. "The Incomparable Rozalyn Maxwell" was performing this weekend. "Home from her Triumphant Tour of Asia."

"And of Helen Robins's dungeon." I smiled to myself as I realized that I was now privy to one of the great secrets of the world. I looked at the picture next to her billing. Yes, it was the Roz I'd always known with big glittering earrings, beautifully done makeup, and a sparkling gown. I sighed and smiled. Ah, if the world only knew.

Still sore but in a better mood than when I was obsessing about the pain in my butt, I sauntered on, trying to decide what to buy as a treat for having at least survived last night.

❖

I'd only been home a few minutes, long enough to spread my new purchases on my bed, when I heard the key in the front door. Going down the small hallway to the living room door, I peered in to make sure it was Helen.

"Good evening, Mistress. Did the recording session go well?" I asked as she tossed her purse and briefcase onto the couch.

"Hi, Little Butch." She smiled weakly. "The session went well, but it was draining." She sank down onto her black chair.

"Can I get you a drink?"

She sighed. "That would be wonderful." She let her head fall back onto the chair. As I took down a glass, she said, "Make yourself one, too, if you like."

I turned in surprise. "Thank you, Mistress." I smiled, then took down a second glass. With two drinks, one the usual vodka on ice with a twist, the other a rum and ginger ale, I walked back to her and handed her the vodka.

"Sit down," she said.

I started to sit on the floor, but before I could sink far, she took my arm. "Sit on the couch."

Surprised, I sat on the couch. Had something happened? As I tasted my drink, I watched her carefully. She looked very tired. I adjusted myself. It still felt as if I was sitting on a handful of marbles.

Helen laughed as she studied me. "How is your bottom today?"

I smiled. "Tender, very tender."

"Let me see."

I took a gulp of my drink, then set it on the floor and slowly peeled my jeans down with my panties and bent over, ass toward her.

I heard her gasp and looked at my panties. They were smeared with blood.

She touched me gently. "This one needs to be butterflied," she said, more to herself than to me. "And a couple of these welts are swollen with blood. They should be lanced before they fester and cause permanent damage." She stood. "Come on, Little Butch, first aid time."

She walked across the room as I pulled my pants to just below my ass, picked up my drink, and followed her. It seemed strange to be following her into the dungeon rather than waiting for her there. As we entered, she went into the bathroom for the medicine cabinet and ran water in the sink. Not knowing what to do, I let my jeans drop and stepped out of them.

"Take all your clothes off," she called. "Let me see what other damage we did." The water stopped running as I hung my shirt on the hook behind the door. "Come on over here," she said, coming out of the bathroom carrying a tray of bottles and bandages. She set the tray on the equipment table next to her drink, then turned the light switch so that it was much brighter. It felt wrong to have it that bright in there.

I turned slowly as she signaled.

"Stop." She touched the black and blue finger marks on my hip. "Do these hurt?"

"Not very much."

She touched a few other bruises. I just sighed. There wasn't much to say. "Well, at least it's not as bad as I feared. You're lucky only four of those lashes broke skin. Roz loves to draw blood. Only this one, where it crosses the other, looks deep enough to be concerned. It should have been stitched, but I think a good butterfly will close it. There shouldn't be any permanent damage. How in hell did you sit on the blood blisters today?"

"It wasn't easy." I shrugged.

She pointed to the horse. "Better brace yourself. This will not be pleasant pain."

I stretched over the horse as she went back to the tray. By the brighter light, I could see how sweat had tarnished the metal handles on the far side of the horse. They were much dingier than I remembered. I made a note to polish them the next time I cleaned the dungeon.

"I'm surprised you had the strength to clean up in here this morning. Did you go to a movie?" Helen said.

"No, ma'am. I went shopping in the Village."

"Shopping," Helene said in wonder. "How did you have the strength? You amaze me. Most boys would have stayed in bed all day after half of what you took last night."

I felt pride in her voice. "I bought some new shirts. I hope you like them."

"Low cut?"

"Yes, ma'am."

"I'll like them." The cold of alcohol glided gently across my butt. I winced as it burned some of the welts. "It's going to take some time for these to heal properly, for the swelling to go down," Helen murmured. "We'll have to find something soft for you to sit on for a few days." She laughed. "And some other part of your body to abuse."

"Yes, Mistress." I smiled. "Whatever pleases you."

"Such a good boy," she said, patting my hip. Then her voice turned serious. "I'm going to let some of this blood drain to bring the swelling down. Otherwise, it'll leave damage. That would be horrible for such a pretty little bottom. This will hurt for just a moment. Be very still."

I felt a jab as her scalpel sliced into me. I gripped the handles as warm blood trickled down my leg.

"Another," she said. This jab didn't hurt half as much. "And the last."

I shuddered as she pressed the welts to squeeze the remaining blood.

"You all right?" she asked.

"Yes, ma'am."

"Good," she said, "because this is going to really hurt. And you don't have to be brave this time, Little Butch. I'm not enjoying this."

I almost screamed as she wiped the cuts with a cool liquid, probably mercurochrome or some other antiseptic. I sighed deeply as she wiped up the blood with a warm wet towel. Then she handed me a washcloth, and I wiped the tears from my eyes.

"I'll butterfly all of these so they won't need stitches. I don't think they'll leave scars, but we'll keep an eye on them. If they bother you, let me know."

"Yes, ma'am." I sighed as she applied tape to the cuts.

She was slow and meticulous. Then she spread a wide strip of gauze over the cuts and taped it in place.

I drew a quick breath as she spread my ass cheeks carefully. At least it didn't feel like someone was going to tear me apart. "How does this feel today? Any bleeding?"

"Not that I noticed," I answered, taking a deep breath. It hurt, but not nearly as badly as before. "But I had a little stinging when I went to the bathroom."

"There's a small tear," she said, "Did you clean it well?"

"Yes, ma'am. I took a warm bath with Epsom salts."

"That helped some, but you still have to watch yourself carefully." She turned back to the table. "This will help." She spread a cool, smooth salve on my asshole. Then she stepped back. "That should do it for now. Let me know if anything feels wrong or if the swelling or pain doesn't go right away. One of those blood blisters was like a rock. It has me concerned."

"Yes, ma'am," I said as I pushed back from the horse.

As I turned, she handed me an ice pack. "Hold this against your bottom for a while. It'll help the swelling."

I took the ice pack and leaned against the horse to hold it in place. I sighed deeply. The pain wasn't nearly as bad as it had been, and the coolness from the ice felt soothing.

I looked up to see Helen watching me. She touched my collar. "Did you wear this shopping today?"

"Yes, ma'am," I said. "I'm sorry. I couldn't, I didn't want to take it off. It would have felt like I was disconnecting from you, and I didn't want that."

"Did anyone say anything about it?"

I smiled, a little self-consciously. "I got a couple strange looks."

Helen shook her head. "How did it feel?"

"I wished I could have told them about you."

She pulled her stool over and sat. The look on her face was

quite serious. After a minute, she said, "I have to apologize for last night."

I started to object, but she put up her hand.

"No. It was wrong, especially on your very first night with a locked collar. I failed you. It should never have happened like that." She took a deep breath. "It's never all right for a dominatrix to allow her submissive to be harmed like you were." She sighed. "I knew that Roz was going too far, and I knew that you were in distress. I should have stopped it, but I let it get out of hand. I truly apologize. You have every right to take off that collar and walk out the door."

"Mistress, I'd never walk out on you. I was the one who failed. I yelled my safe word!"

Helen shook her head. "If you hadn't, you'd probably be in the hospital right now. Our contract was for me to protect you and you to serve me. You gave me the best of service last night, and I let you down. I didn't protect you. I broke the contract." She shifted, crossing her legs and leaning forward. "Roz is very much the sadist and a very passionate woman. We've known each other for years, but we could never be together because I won't take her abuse. I think you could tell there's a certain love between us, but we also respect each other's needs and desires. What happened last night was partly my desire to see her pleased. You got caught in the middle. I'm very sorry."

I watched in silence as her face changed expressions several times. I knew she was having a hard time putting what she had to say into words. I'd never seen this part of her and could tell that this very personal side was not something she was used to talking about.

"You must love each other a great deal," I offered. I felt privileged to be privy to that connection.

She smiled sadly. "Perhaps." Then she smiled broadly.

"And you showed a great deal of love for me last night. When a boy has to use his safe word, you expect tears. But they're usually from the pain or humiliation. Your tears were because you thought you'd embarrassed me. It was a remarkable response. You made me very proud." She nodded, laughing. "Roz was so shocked she nearly peed her pants. I don't think either of us has ever seen a sub react like that. And believe me, we've heard a lot of subs yell their safe words." She reached for my hand. "I was stunned. And truly honored. I promise you, Little Butch, my Mickey Mouth, I will never let anything like that ever happen again. Please accept my apology."

Tears rolled down my face. I fell to my knees and wrapped my arms around her legs, laying my head on her lap. The only words I could think right then were, "I adore you." I let my feelings float out around me as she gently, lovingly stroked my hair.

CHAPTER SIXTEEN

I'd just come back from running errands, my arms full of laundry and a few groceries. Helen was seated on the couch next to a very light-skinned black woman who I judged to be about thirty or thirty-five. They were deep in conversation, so I went into the kitchen to put the groceries away.

Helen called after me. "Would you make some coffee?"

"Right away," I answered and set the old percolator to boiling. I brought the laundry into the living room to take it upstairs.

"I'll take that." Helen held out her hands for the package, then went up the stairs. I was surprised she hadn't told me to take it up.

"You must be Mickey," a voice said from the couch. "I'm Tina. I suspect she's told me a lot more about you than she's told you about me." She flashed a warm smile. My insecurity took over. Was this a new conquest of Helen's? Someone with the potential to replace me?

Tina must have read the expression on my face. "She never tells anyone about me. Next to you, I'm the best kept secret in town. And you've nothing to worry about." She smiled a very beguiling grin. "I'm Helen's daughter."

"Her daughter?"

Tina laughed, a Helen gesture. "Yes. My dear parents thought it would be better to keep me out of the limelight in case someone found out about my mother's other hobbies."

"I didn't even know she had children." I was amazed.

"Just me. Daddy died when I was eight. He was her first agent."

I nodded, letting this new information start to sink in. Of course. There was the picture of the handsome, gray-haired white man on the table in her bedroom. I'd always wondered who that was.

"Where's Jackie?" Helen asked, coming back down the stairs.

"Zabar's," Tina answered. "Where else?" She directed her next remark at me. "We get into New York once every other month, and the first place my daughter has to go to is a gourmet food store. Jackie is definitely her grandmother's granddaughter. It scares me sometimes."

I looked at Helen. She had a granddaughter, too? This was almost too much to comprehend.

"Don't believe a word she says," Helen told me. "I found her in an alley and made the mistake of giving her something to eat. Now I can't get rid of her, and she goes around spreading vicious lies about being my daughter."

Tina laughed. "You can't deny me, Mom. I have the same sense of humor as you."

"But you have your father's musical talent...which was nonexistent."

"At least I know good music when I hear it." She looked at me. "Mom made sure I got a good musical education."

"Someone had to," Helen said.

The warm banter felt good. Maybe I'd learn something about the enigma that was still Helen Robins. I looked at them closely, trying to spot similarities. Then I remembered the coffee and looked at my watch. "Oops, the coffee should be done. I hope you like it strong."

"Just like my men," Tina answered as I started for the kitchen. "Strong, hot, and black."

"There'll be no dirty talk in this house, young lady," Helen said.

Hearing them made me smile. They definitely had the same laugh. As I brought out the coffee, the door flew open, and a teenager bounced in carrying two large Zabar's shopping bags. It was a miniature Helen Robins. The smile, the eyes, and the way she moved were all the image of her grandmother.

"Hi, Granny!" She smiled, giving Helen a quick kiss.

Helen cringed. "Haven't I told you not to call me that? I said I'd give you five dollars to call me Helen."

Jackie looked at Helen as only a teenager can. "Helen, Helen, Helen, Helen, Helen, Helen, Helen. There, now you've just paid for the food I bought at Zabar's. I charged it to your account."

"You'd better get her under control," Helen said to Tina. "One of these days, I might not laugh."

"That's between you two." Tina shrugged. "I'm staying out of the crossfire."

Jackie held out her hand to me. "Hi, I'm Jackie. You must be Helen's new trick."

I looked at Helen, shocked. This child couldn't be more than fourteen. Where had she learned things like that?

Helen just shrugged. "Out of the mouths of babes…"

Tina laughed. "Don't look at me. I'm just her mother. Her grandmother is responsible for that part of her education."

"What? Am I right or not?" Jackie looked back at me. "You live here with Helen, right? And she plays with you in her dungeon."

"Jackie, I think there are better ways of phrasing that,"

Helen said, looking as if she was trying to suppress a smile. I felt shaken.

"I apologize," Tina said. "I moved to West Chester to keep her away from the bad influence of her grandmother, but it didn't seem to work."

I didn't know how to respond to any of this. How long had this been going on? Why didn't anyone know about this?

"Maybe we'd better take your purchases into the kitchen. It's getting too hot in here. The food will spoil." Helen steered Jackie out of the room.

After watching them go, Tina turned to me. "I do apologize. She's very precocious. Sometimes she really oversteps her boundaries."

"It's all right," I assured her as I sank onto one of the red chairs. "I just wasn't prepared. I guess you just have to call them as you see them."

"Still..." Tina shook her head. "Mom has spoiled her rotten. Jackie wandered into the dungeon when she was ten. Mom's never been one to cushion the truth. I think it took Jackie all of three hours to learn what each and every one of Mom's toys was used for. I'm never certain which one of them I'm supposed to be the mother of and which one I'm a daughter to."

"It's fine. Living with Helen has taken a lot of getting used to. I'm usually not shocked by anything anymore."

"You seem to be making her happy."

"Thank you." I almost blushed.

Helen came back into the room. "When are you going to teach your daughter the value of money?" she demanded. "Even I don't shell out twenty-three dollars a pound for imported prosciutto!"

"You're the one who thought your granddaughter should appreciate the finer things in life."

Helen scowled at her, then me. "And you can keep that Mickey Mouth grin off your face, or I'll see you upstairs at 9:03 tonight."

I swallowed hard, trying to keep from smiling.

"Is she still using that old intimidation routine?" Tina laughed. "She used to do that to me. You be home by 11:09, young lady, or you're grounded for a week." A wide smile lit her face. "Of course, I don't suppose she grounds you, does she?"

"No." I had to laugh. "I wouldn't call it grounding. Grinding, maybe. But not grounding."

Tina shook her head. "As much as I've lived with it, I still don't understand the attraction. Of course, that's Mom's big disappointment in life. Mistress Helen raised a straight vanilla girl."

Helen gave her shoulder a warm nudge. "Out of all the things I could be disappointed in, that isn't one of them. Your father would have been proud of you. He couldn't understand it either." Helen looked at me. "I loved her father. We were just never good in bed together."

"Must have been at least once." I grinned. "Or she wouldn't be here."

"That's it, Mickey Mouth. 9:07."

I bowed my eyes as I heard an enthusiastic, "Great! Can I watch?"

"No!" two voices said in unison.

Looking up, I caught a very amused look in Helen's eyes.

"No, you may not," Tina said rapidly.

"Oh, Mom. You're no fun at all!"

Helen broke out in a laugh as she reached for her Shermans. I jumped to grab the lighter and held it out for her. "She's right, you know." She stared at Tina. "I've told you that a hundred times."

Tina let out a deep sigh of resignation. "Now I get it from both sides."

"Isn't that what makes you fun?" I asked in all seriousness.

Helen started to laugh but burst out into one of her coughing fits.

"Haven't you given up those things yet?" Tina asked. "You know they're gonna kill you one of these days."

Helen harrumphed. "It'll take more than one of these to kill *this* broad." She smiled, tapping herself on her chest. "Besides, why should I stop doing something that makes me happy? Haven't I taught you that life is more important than that? Even your father understood that."

"I know, Mom, but you know how I worry."

"I've told you enough times; if these are gonna kill me they should have done it by now. I've been smoking so long it's much too late to back off."

Tina turned to me. "Can't you hide these things? How can you let her smoke that shit?"

"I have nothing to do with it." I tried to distance myself from what sounded like a long-running feud. Tina just shook her head and gave up.

CHAPTER SEVENTEEN

As the weeks wore on, life seemed very simple. I finished transcribing all the tapes, and Helen was finishing the last rewrites. As I watched her make the corrections to the scores, I realized how deeply in love I was. Each stroke of her pencil across the paper made me yearn for the stroke across my skin. Our days had become serene and quiet. We'd do our own work silently and shared the space with a gentleness that radiated comfort. I was in heaven.

"How long do you think it will take you to redo these pages and transpose the sax parts?"

I almost didn't hear the question.

"Are you asleep, Little Butch?"

"I'm sorry," I said sheepishly. "I guess I was daydreaming. Let me take a look." I reached for the manuscript and looked through the pages. "About three days."

Helen sat back in her red leather chair. "You amaze me."

I lowered my eyes, warmed by her compliment.

"I'll schedule a reading for the week after next. If it goes well and I don't decide to do many rewrites, we can schedule a performance for that week I'm at the Cookery in mid-September."

"Mid-September?" I hadn't even thought that far in advance. "That's only a few weeks!"

"Yes." She smiled. "I didn't think it would be finished before I left. You've done a miraculous job."

"Me?" I said in awe. "It's your music." My head was swimming, but my stomach began to turn. I'd forgotten that Helen was scheduled to go on a five-week tour in the fall. Well, not forgotten, just trying to hope it'd go away. I didn't want to think of five weeks without her.

"It's my music, but you brought it to life. It would have stayed on those tapes for the rest of my life if you hadn't written it down. It wouldn't ever be heard if it wasn't for you." She studied me as I searched for words to respond. "Come over here and kiss me."

I was shocked to hear those words, but I rushed to obey. I knelt beside her and leaned up to kiss her cheek, but she turned, and our lips met. I kissed her tentatively, but she pulled me to her and kissed me deeply, passionately. Her tongue pushed into my mouth, and I was swept away with the power of her embrace.

Never before had I ever been so overwhelmed by a kiss. I felt as if I was falling into her. Her tongue, her lips, her breath mesmerized me. I was awash in a sea of feelings so intense, I thought I was going to float away.

Helen at last pulled back. "Let's go upstairs," she whispered. Taking my hand, she led me. I started for the door of the dungeon, but she stopped me. "Not tonight, Mickey." She smiled. I was stunned. She never used my real name. But she took my hand and led me to her room.

I had peeked into her room before when she wasn't home, but I'd never trespassed. I'd been forbidden from entering, and it never occurred to me to disobey. I stopped at the door, hesitant.

"Come on in, Little Butch." I couldn't read the look in her

eyes. She threw back the white satin bedspread and turned, holding out her hand.

That night I saw another side of Helen Robins. She made love to me in her own bed, roughly, as I'd expected, but with a sweetness I hadn't anticipated.

And she allowed me, at last, to make love to her. I feasted on her body, worshipping each and every inch of her, at last coming to rest at that one place I truly adored. I continued for hours until I felt her shudder, and she reached down to bring my face up to hers.

That night, I slept in the arms of Helen Robins, surrounded by her warmth, her fragrance, and her love.

❖

Helen and her band—Joe on bass and Dennis on drums—rehearsed for hours at the studio. At night, if the rehearsal had gone well, we'd spend time together, sometimes in the dungeon, more often listening to tapes of the rehearsal.

But time was scarce. There was a sense of urgency as the days passed, phone calls to make, rehearsals to schedule, details to see to. Even though it wouldn't be a full performance with four horns and six backup singers as Helen had scored it, it still took on a life of its own. Johnny Williams was already rehearsing, and Roz Maxwell would come into town to do the other vocals. Helen had also arranged for Stephen to come down from Boston to play a couple of the saxophone solos.

I looked at Helen as she hung up the phone. The first of the four performances in the small Midtown club was only three days away. She looked at me and sighed deeply. "Roz sends her love, Little Butch. She's looking forward to seeing you again."

I swallowed. "Seeing me?"

Helen roared with laughter. "You didn't think she'd forget you, did you? She's tried very hard to get me to loan you out or sell you to her."

I swallowed hard. Was I starting to sweat? "Would you do that?"

Helen just studied me for a moment. "No. Do you want me to loan you to Roz? That decision's yours."

I felt as if I was being squeezed in a trap. "N...no," I stammered. "I think once was enough."

"Are you sure?"

"Do you want to loan me to Roz?"

Helen sat back, her eyes unreadable. "You made a big impression on her. She's a very powerful dom in this lifestyle. She could do a lot for you...both in a dungeon and in a recording studio."

I sank to my knees. "You give me everything I want."

Helen placed her hand on my cheek. "But I can't add to your piano career. You'd be in direct competition to me." She smiled. "You might even replace me in history."

"Oh, never, never. I could never replace you. No one will ever be able to replace the great Helen Robins."

"Oh." Helen sat back, laughing, "You are so slick! You always have the right things to say, don't you, my Mickey Mouth? One of these days, that mouth of yours is going to get you into big trouble."

"Only for you," I whispered, my head bowed, not just in submission but to hide the smile.

I could feel her leering at me. "8:57, Little Butch. Thirty-four minutes."

Chapter Eighteen

I paced for hours as the rehearsal dragged on. I'd have thought it was my music that was going to be born the next night. Every time there was a pause, a mistake, a hiccup in the music, I'd search my score and make notes. I made sure that each correction, addition, or change Helen wanted was noted so that I could correct the final score.

Johnny's deep baritone roared out the music. It was exactly as I had heard it in my head, precisely as Helen had written it. And Sir Roz was spectacular. The music had been written just for her, and she sang it with every bit of her expertise, as if she'd lived with it for years.

During a break, as Helen was discussing one of the solos with Stephen, Roz ambled up to where I was busy making my notes. "Well, well. You certainly must have ears of steel." She laughed. "I was amazed when Helen sent me the full score. That's quite a piece of work you've done."

"Thank you, sir," I murmured, my eyes lowered.

She laughed. "Call me Miss Maxwell, dear. We're in public," she said in a very conspiratorial voice.

"I'm sorry…Miss Maxwell."

She shook her head. "Tell me, do you ever write your own music?"

"I have written a bit, but it isn't anything like this."

"No, I guess nothing is. I'm surprised you've found any time at all with all this going on."

"Well, it helps when I've been listening to the tapes for too long, and I can't hear anything anymore. At least I can write just what I hear in my head."

"If you've got anything you think I'd sound good with, send me a copy. I'd like to see it."

"Thank you. I think you'd sound wonderful with anything." I kept my eyes lowered, feeling her stare pierce me. To have someone like Roz sing my work? That could put my name on the map.

"Don't tell your mistress you said that." She winked. "It might make her jealous."

I shook my head. "She knows I love her."

"Yes, she does." With that, she walked away to talk to Dennis and Joe.

"Okay, let's run that last duet one more time," Helen's called. As everyone took their places, Helen said to me, "I think we've got this baby just about wrapped up. What do you think?"

"It's spectacular. It's everything you wanted."

"Really?" Helen looked at me thoughtfully. "Do me a favor? Play the piano part this time. I want to hear it from out front." Without waiting for my answer, she turned. "Okay, everyone, take it from letter L. I want to hear the finale. If it goes well, I think we can put it to rest until tomorrow night. You've all worked so very hard. I'm very pleased."

As I slid onto the piano bench, everyone looked from Helen to me.

"Everyone ready?" she asked. "Let's do it."

Without hesitation, Dennis counted into the piece.

I don't remember playing, but the music soared. It felt as

if Helen was using my hands, and I waited just above, playing exactly what she wanted as she used me the way she used me in the dungeon, to do her every wish, to fulfill her desires. I felt her power surging through me, and at that moment, I was totally hers. I belonged to her just as much as the music did. She'd written me, too.

The opera rolled to its climax as if urged to the ultimate orgasm. As Stephen's sax sobbed its soul out, Roz's voice hit notes I didn't realize she had. As the music faded to its final release, stunned silence filled the room.

Then raucous applause broke out. All of the bartenders and waiters setting up for the night's crowd stopped and cheered. But the loudest of all was Helen.

"Yes! Yes!" she crowed. "That's it. That's just it!"

I realized that the sound of the applause had changed, and as I looked up, still in a stupor, I realized everyone was looking at me. And applauding. I glanced at Helen, embarrassed. The applause should have been hers, not mine. But Helen was looking at me, too, a satisfied smile on her face. She hugged me tightly.

"That was wonderful," she whispered. "How does 10:08 sound?" And then she turned away to thank and congratulate everyone for their hard work.

Stephen was at my side. "That was phenomenal. And everyone thought you just moved to New York to get laid." He laughed as he started to take his sax apart. "You know, I always knew you were good...at playing the piano."

I shook my head.

"You got time for a bite to eat?" he asked.

"Not tonight, Steve, I'm exhausted. Besides, I'm sure Helen will have some changes to be made."

"Yeah, she's quite a taskmaster, isn't she?"

I couldn't help but chuckle. As he walked away, I looked

up to see Roz leaning against the piano. There was a moment of silence as she stared at me. Finally, she laughed. "Helen's really done a wonderful job with you, hasn't she? If she ever throws you out, give me a call. I could use someone with your talents…in many ways."

"What's happening here? Are you intimidating my boy again?" Helen chuckled softly as she came up to us.

"No, darling, not intimidating. Just pointing out some options. Where's the food tonight?"

"There's dinner waiting at home. You are coming over for a while, aren't you?"

"Sure." Roz smiled, looking at me. "What's for dessert?"

Helen smiled. "Oh, we'll find something sweet."

Roz turned to me, nodding. "Yes, I think we will. If we can take it upstairs."

Helen looked at me. "What do you say to that?"

I hesitated. Again? Could I refuse? Did I want to? Would I be able to redeem myself from last time? Would I be able to outlast Sir Roz? "If that's what you wish, ma'am."

Roz's face broke out into a wide smile. She turned to Helen. "You are such a wonderful hostess, darling. How can I ever repay you?" She turned toward the other musicians.

Helen smiled broadly. "Are you sure this is all right with you?" she asked, not taking her eyes off Roz.

I wet my lips. "I think I can do this. I'll try. Now that I know what to expect, I'll try…for you."

"Last time, you did it for me. This time, it has to be for yourself." She looked deeply into my eyes. "Only if you're sure. You can always say no. I'll make excuses to Roz."

"I'll be okay. You'll be there, won't you?"

"Yes, sweet boy, I'll be right there. Every second. I promise."

CHAPTER NINETEEN

Dinner was wonderful as always. Rachel had left veal chops seasoned and waiting to be put under the broiler. There were also garlic mashed potatoes and an assortment of vegetables. It made everyone happy. As I served Helen and Roz coffee, Helen gave a deep sigh and leaned back in her chair.

"This has been such a wonderful day!" She turned to Roz. "And I am so very glad you're here. Are you sure you won't move back to New York?"

"Oh no, not me. I love California too much." Roz chuckled, then turned to me. "Have you ever been to LA?"

"No, sir. I've never been off the East Coast."

"Well, you'll have to come west, boy. And bring this old broad with you if you want." She laughed, pointing her thumb at Helen.

"Old broad? Who're you calling an old broad, you old broad!"

Roz let out a loud laugh. Helen just smiled at her. "I've never been called an old broad." Roz laughed, looking at me. "An old fart a couple times."

"I bet I could still make you scream uncle," Helen countered.

"Maybe, maybe not," Roz said with a sly smile. "Why don't we see what the boy screams? Then you can work on me."

"Uh." I backpedaled. "Don't get me in the middle of this."

"You already are," Helen said without taking her eyes off Roz. Then she looked at her watch. "Besides, you have dishes to do. And 10:08 isn't that far away. You'd better get to work."

"Yes, ma'am," I said as I brought the tray of dirty dishes back into the kitchen. I'd have to do a lot of thinking while I did the dishes to get into the mindset to deal with tonight. The dungeon would be so very different from the rehearsal hall.

❖

Kneeling in the dungeon, waiting, I started to shake. I'd been here before, hadn't I? And I hadn't been able to handle Roz's sadism. How was I going to handle it this time?

Of course, that was a long time ago. I had more experience now, didn't I? I could handle more…and I liked it more. The pain was much more pleasurable now. The more pain, the more pleasure. Helen and Master Lawrence had taught me how to handle it. And now, at least, I knew what to expect from Roz. Or did I? I took a big sigh. Could I succeed this time, or would I safe word out again? Why had I said yes?

I heard the door open and froze, my back straight, my head up, my eyes down, and my hands firmly clasped behind my back.

"Worried, boy?" It was Helen.

"Yes, ma'am." I sighed.

She put her hand on my shoulder. "Don't be. You have your caution word if it starts to get too rough. That'll slow things down. And you have your safe word that will stop everything. But you're a lot stronger than you were the last time. And Roz respects you. Everything will go well. You'll be fine." She sat on her stool.

"Thank you, Mistress," I whispered, wishing I could be as confident as she was.

"Don't worry, boy. There's always tomorrow."

"Sure, if I live that long."

Just then, the door opened. I knew it was Roz. She'd changed into her butch drag; I saw the heavy men's shoes striding around me. "Is he ready?"

"Yes. I think so," Helen answered, standing to greet her.

"Just wait till I show you these new clips I bought in San Francisco." Roz sneered, letting a large black leather bag drop to the ground. "Can we tie him to the wall?"

"I don't think that'll be necessary." I heard the proud smile in Helen's voice. "This boy has learned a lot of discipline. I haven't had to tie him down in months."

"Really? More impressive every day."

"Where do you want him?"

"How about against that wall?"

"You heard him, boy."

"Yes, ma'am. Thank you," I said, taking a deep breath and making my way to the platform against the wall, remembering to stay on my knees and keep my back straight, my hands clasped behind me.

When I had reached the platform, I crawled up and stopped. I could feel Roz behind me. "Stand. Turn around."

"Yes, sir. Thank you, sir." I stood and turned my back to the wall.

Roz studied me. "You sure you can take this without being tied?"

"If it's all right with you, sir. Whatever you want, sir."

Had I really said that? Where had that popped into my mouth from? Whatever Sir Roz wanted? I hoped I hadn't just put myself into something I couldn't handle.

"Well, maybe you should hang on to the chains," Roz said lowering the tethers from the ceiling. She adjusted my grasp until I was stretched wide. I gripped them tightly.

"Now, don't let go. I wouldn't want to have to punish you for dropping them. Do you understand me?"

"Yes, sir."

"Good." She opened the black bag. "Helen, look at these. Have you ever seen anything so marvelous?"

Helen and Roz hovered over the bag. I didn't want to look. I figured I'd know about them soon enough. Helen had used locking tweezers on me before, and the sting was incredible, both when they were put on and when they were taken off, allowing the feeling to rush back into the pinched flesh.

"Are you watching, boy?"

At Roz's words, I opened my eyes, which I hadn't even known I'd closed, and looked up. In her hands were wooden clamps with big metal jaws covered with thin leather and large springs holding them closed. I don't know what the look on my face was, but it must have been fear because Roz broke out in a loud laugh and turned to Helen.

"Maybe I won't have to use these. He'll pass out just thinking of what they'll feel like." She turned back to me. "Are you sure you can take these without dropping those shackles?"

I took a very difficult and deep swallow. It seemed as if all the moisture in my mouth had disappeared. "Yes, sir."

"Helen," Roz called over her shoulder, not taking her eyes off me, "I got these from a friend in the Castro who works with electric devices. Look how nicely these hold."

With that, she started applying the clamps, one by one, not more than a quarter inch apart up both of my arms, across my chest, and down my torso. After a few minutes of intense pain, it all started to even out and became manageable, almost pleasant. Yes, I could maintain this without accepting the pain as bad.

"What do you think, Helen?" Roz asked.

"Very artistic, very nice. Are you okay, boy?"

I wasn't sure where I was. I heard everything they were saying, but I felt a mile away. I could feel each and every one of the clips, but the pain had faded hours ago. Or minutes. However long it had been.

Helen touched my face. That brought me back into the dungeon. "Little Butch?"

"Yes, ma'am," I managed.

"Are you okay?"

"Yes, ma'am."

"Can we continue?" Roz asked.

"Yes, please, sir," I answered, remembering my manners.

Roz and Helen both laughed evilly. "Then maybe we should try these. What do you think, darling?" Roz held up a bunch of clamps strung together on a long black cord.

Helen smirked. "I think he'll really like those. Probably too much. You may have to send me some of those when you get back to California."

Roz started to clip the clamps on my breasts, circling around and around toward my nipples. I watched as she worked. I was amazed at her artistry. She seemed to know exactly where to place each one and just how long the cords would reach so that the very last one on each end of the cord just reached my nipples. But she left the last ones off, holding them out in front of me.

"You ready for this, boy?" she asked.

I watched her from so far away, I wasn't even aware of answering, but I must have nodded.

"Then here we go." With that, she let the final two snap on my nipples.

Next I knew, Helen wiped my face with a soft cloth. "Amazing. He didn't even let go of the chains."

Blinking, I looked up. I still held on to the tethers, but I had fallen to my knees.

"Very pretty, Roz. It almost looks like he's feathered. I'm always amazed at your creativity."

They talked about the clamps for a few minutes. Or maybe it was hours. Time had lost its meaning. I was aware when Roz stood in front of me holding a long, thin black cane.

She helped me to my feet. "Are you ready for them to come off?"

"Yes, sir," I answered automatically.

I wasn't ready for the cane to come down on the row of clamps on my left arm. Several flew in the air. As the blood and feeling rushed to the places where the clamps had been, a sharp stab of pain replaced the numbness. A loud moan escaped my lips.

Then another snap of the cane flipped clamps off my right arm. A third snap removed more from my left arm, then another on my right. Several snaps across my chest ripped the single clamps from there. One after another, Roz flicked the clamps off. Soon, I was so encircled by pain, I could hardly stand. My entire concentration was tied into standing and holding on to the chains. Could I live through this? Would I pass out? All I knew was the sting of pain going up one arm, across my chest, and on to the other arm. I gripped at the chains, knowing that I had to hang on. If nothing else, they were my lifeline.

Roz proceeded to rip the clamps off my stomach and

sides. Soon all that remained were the ones around my beasts, the ones strung together by the long black cords.

"How are you doing, boy?" Helen's voice pushed its way through the web of pain.

I fought to push myself above the surface. "I'm...I'm here...ma'am."

"Good boy. Such a good boy." She stroked my face. "Just a little more. We're almost done."

"Yes, ma'am. Thank you, ma'am." I felt as if my voice was scratching its way through tons of sand.

"Here. Sip this."

Helen raised a glass to my lips, and I took a sip of cold liquid. I was beyond identifying the taste. It could have been water or soda or even carrot juice.

"Ready?" Roz asked, taking the black cord that hung between my breasts. I just stared at her as she glared into my eyes and stepped back.

The world erupted in a blaze of red and black as Roz ripped the cord away, stripping the clamps from around my breasts so quickly that it all became a blur. I'd never felt this much pain before, not even the last time I'd been in Roz's hands. This was just color, pain, and the sound of my own screams.

The only thing that kept me upright was the chains. My legs had become water; my knees buckled under me.

"I sure hope you have this room soundproofed well," Roz said through the haze.

"Well, no one's called the police yet, so it must be well dampened." She touched my chest. My breathing was ragged, but I fought to calm it and willed my knees to straighten.

"Do you still have that nasty glove?" Roz asked. "Some of these marks look like they're just begging to bleed."

I looked at my chest as Helen went to the armoire. She

returned with a black leather glove and a bottle of alcohol. It looked like a regular glove until I pulled myself into consciousness. Then I realized what Helen held. The fingers looked as if someone had stuck thumbtacks through from the inside so each finger was a row of sharp points.

Helen slipped the glove over her right hand and held it out. Then she placed her hand on my chest above my left breast. Without taking her eyes off mine, she leaned in. Each little tack pulled at my flesh. I closed my eyes.

"Don't zone out on me yet, Little Butch," Helen whispered as she took her hand away.

I looked down. My breast was covered with small red dots, a few oozing blood.

"Is the other one jealous?" she asked as she slapped my right breast, not waiting for an answer.

I gasped, starting to shake. I hung on to the chains tighter.

"And he's not even thanking you for that glorious blood, Helen. I thought he'd be more grateful than that," Roz voice boomed through the haze again.

I knew there was something I wanted to say but wasn't sure what it was.

"Are you okay, my Little Butch?"

It took me a minute to think of an answer. "Yes, ma'am. Thank you, Mistress. I'm…grateful."

I heard Roz roar. Helen placed her hand on my head and forced my head back. "Look me in the eyes, boy, and repeat that."

I had to search for a moment to focus on her. "Thank you, Mistress," I repeated. What else had I said? "I'm…I'm grateful for your…your…" I stopped, trying to remember.

"My what? Where are you focused, boy?"

"Your pain, ma'am."

"What about my pain?" Helen seemed to smile.

"Thank you for giving me pain, ma'am." Had I said it right? My mind wasn't working as well as it should have.

"Very good, my boy." Helen patted her glove down my torso, one side and then the other, coaxing blood from many of the red, swollen marks Roz's clamps had left.

"Very nice, darling," Roz said. "He bleeds so nicely."

Helen smeared the oozing blood across my chest. "Want to see how good that tastes?" she asked as she offered her hand. I started to suck her fingers, tasting the metallic, salty taste. I began to suckle, my eyes closed, my head spinning.

Finally, Helen placed her hand on my forehead, and I looked into her face. "Zoning, aren't you, boy." She smiled.

I couldn't even formulate an answer. I just blinked. She started to unwrap my hand from around the chain. "I think you need to sit down. Can you do that?" she asked.

I nodded. She and Roz helped me sink to the floor. I sprawled, my back against the wall, my mind a blur, staring at the smear of blood across my body. I didn't know how long I remained there before I realized that Roz was sitting on the floor with me.

We just sat there, looking at each other. I hadn't even noticed Helen had left until the door opened, and she came back. "How's he doing?" she asked.

Roz chuckled. "I think he's coming back to life. He certainly has a deep zone, doesn't he?"

"You should see him fly with wax."

"Oh, yes, I'd love to see that."

I gasped. Were we going to try wax now? "Boston?" I ventured.

"Take it easy, Little Butch." Helen smiled. "There's just one other small thing tonight. We'll leave wax for now."

I let my head fall back against the wall, relieved that this was almost over.

Helen kneeled. "This is something I've been planning for a while. It'll commemorate all the work you've done on my music. And how much you've pleased me. I think you're in a good space to accept it tonight."

She set a small tray on the floor. I tried to focus but gave up before I saw more than a bottle and some needles. Helen lit a small candle. It seemed like a ritual, with her the priestess and me the offering. Then she wiped her hand across my body again, gathering blood. She offered the blood to me, and I started to suck once again, sinking back into my lower zone.

Roz moved to support me, holding me firm and steady. It was a very reassuring feeling. Helen wiped my earlobe with alcohol and held a cube of ice on it until it became numb. Then she took a large needle and a cork from the tray.

"I'm giving you another token. This one you'll never have to take off when you go out. This will always be with you."

She pierced my ear. Then she opened a small black box. In it was one small stud, a gold music note. Within minutes, the note was clamped on to my ear. She held a mirror up so I could see. "What do you think, boy?"

I moved until it was in focus, a beautiful gold quarter note on my ear. "It's beautiful! Thank you, thank you, Mistress. It's beautiful."

Helen laughed. "Well, you certainly are glib when you're in zone, aren't you?" She put a towel across me so that the blood wouldn't drip on her shirt and pulled me into her arms. Tears began to flow, but these weren't the same as last time; these were tears of joy and gratitude.

She rocked me until my head started to clear.

"He's grown quite a lot in the past few months. I'm jealous, Helen, really jealous. Is there anything he can't do?"

I looked up to see Helen beaming. "I've only found one limit so far."

"A limit? Really? Besides my hands?" Roz seemed amazed.

Helen broke out laughing. "He's afraid of the dark!"

Chapter Twenty

Without thinking, I scratched an itch on my chest. The sharp pain made me smile. I stepped into the shower and let the warm water wash away the dried blood. There were several places where the water and soap stung, but it was nowhere near as bad as it had been the last time Roz had been in town. As I dried myself off, I couldn't help but laugh. I looked like I had chicken pox: Small red marks lined my body and my arms. Under closer inspection, none were deep enough to cause damage, but there were several bruises where Roz's clamps had bit in deeply.

I went down to breakfast to find Roz and Helen sitting over coffee. Roz had spent the night. My heart did a flip-flop as I realized they might have spent the night together. But then, I thought, taking a deep breath, I had no hold over Helen. I was hers; she wasn't mine. That wasn't part of our contract.

"Well, well. How are you this morning?" Helen asked. The look on her face was happy and serene.

"I'm okay. I slept quite soundly."

Roz chuckled. "You were out before we even left the room."

I nodded, a little embarrassed. "I guess I'm not as strong as I think I am."

"You were quite strong last night. I was very proud of you. How are your bruises?" Helen asked.

"I look like I have a wonderful case of the measles," I admitted. Then to Roz, I added, "Those clips were real nasty." I had to smile. "I like them."

Helen looked at Roz. "I told you he would."

Roz just smiled and nodded.

❖

That day, I spent my time running errands, cleaning the dungeon, and making more carrot juice. Roz wouldn't drink it, but Helen chugged it like it was going out of style. Maybe it was the nerves, but she kept to her room, coming out only if she needed something. I found chores to do but was always aware of the sounds that said Helen was up and about or that she wanted something.

Roz worked at the piano. I was amazed at how well she played. It wasn't anything like Helen, but she could hold her own with the best of them. "Whose music is this, boy?" she asked as she thumbed through a pile of work on top of the piano.

"That's mine, sir."

"You wrote this?"

"Yes, sir," I said sheepishly.

"You amaze me, boy," she said, shaking her head. "I'm not sure Helen knows what she has here. How can she keep you locked up with all this talent?"

"She…just can," I stammered, not knowing what to say.

"Don't you want your own career? You could be as famous as Helen."

"I will, sir, when the time is right…when Mistress thinks I'm ready."

"Well, when you are, come see me. I'll make sure you're famous."

"Thank you, sir. I appreciate that."

"I'm not kidding," she assured me.

"About what?" Helen appeared in the doorway.

"About this boy, Helen. He's talented. He needs to be put in the limelight. He should be on a tour of his own."

Helen looked at me. "Is that what you want, boy?"

I wasn't sure what to say. "When I'm ready."

"Helen—" Roz started.

Helen held her hand up. "Do you have errands to run?" she asked me.

I started to say I'd done them all, but from the look in their eyes, I could tell they wanted to talk. "Yes, ma'am. It'll take me about twenty minutes or so. If I might be excused."

"Good boy," she said as I withdrew.

Chapter Twenty-one

I paced outside of the back door of the club. People filed in to hear Helen's music. Some wore very expensive clothing, others didn't, but then, this was New York; almost anything went here.

The day had gone smoothly with both Helen and Roz resting most of the day. All the other performers were here already, sitting with friends in the audience or enjoying a last-minute drink. A small table near the back had been reserved for Roz, Johnny, and Stephen. And me, if I ever felt as if I could sit still. Helen was going over details with Joe and Dennis. They would do one set before the big event. That part was just business as usual for all of them, something they were used to. Helen had admitted to a few butterflies about the opera, but I was more nervous than anyone. They just had to perform; I had to watch.

I had very mixed emotions about this performance. Yes, I'd worked on it for as long as I'd been with Helen, but it meant Helen was that much closer to leaving for her Asian tour.

I hadn't made any plans for her time away. I had a few hints that I'd have some transcribing work from Helen's associates, but nothing had been confirmed. Maybe I'd take some time to go to Boston and visit Frank and some other friends or even take a trip to visit my parents. I hadn't seen them since I'd moved to New York.

"They're gonna start," came a voice behind me, my cue from one of the waitresses.

I slipped inside to the table in back. The place was packed. In fact, the manager was bringing in more chairs. I slid into the seat next to Roz. I noticed Master Lawrence, Robert, and two girls at one of the tables.

Roz must have seen me looking their way. She leaned close. "The Master was asking where you were."

"I'll go over and say hello during intermission." He remembered me? What a privilege.

"I hear you were a very good boy for him while Helen was away."

I smiled. "Thank you, sir."

"Miss Maxwell," she corrected.

I chuckled. "Yes…Miss Maxwell."

Her face broke out in a broad smile. Then Helen and the guys went up onstage. The entire place erupted in applause and cheers. I happily joined in.

Helen acknowledged the recognition, then adjusted the microphone. "We're going to be recording tonight, so you can't be talking during the music, or you'll be on the tape."

Roz leaned in with a smile. "She can't even resist topping a whole audience, can she?"

The music started, and we sat back, smiling broadly. When the set finished, the crowd went wild. I wasn't even the first one on my feet, cheering and howling as the applause erupted, filling the room.

Helen took the microphone as the guys laid their instruments down and started to leave the stage. "All right. We'll be back in a half hour with something special I think you'll like. Rozalyn Maxwell and Johnny Williams will be up here. Until you've heard the two of them together, you haven't heard anything!"

More applause answered her announcement.

"And we have a new sax player I think you'll like. Out of Boston, Mr. Stephen Cogswell. So have a great intermission and a few drinks. Tip your waiters well, and we'll all be back soon." More applause followed her off the stage.

I stood as the waitresses got back in gear to start serving, and conversation rose around the room. Roz was in a discussion with Johnny so I made my way over to Master Lawrence's table and waited until he looked at me.

"Good evening, sir." I smiled. "I hope you're having a good time." I hunkered close to him, hoping that it would pass as a semblance of submission without looking as if I was kneeling.

Lawrence smiled and placed a hand on my shoulder. "Yes, we're having a wonderful time. She's quite something, isn't she?"

"Oh yes, sir. She certainly is."

Robert and the girls added their agreement.

"What's this?" he asked, turning my head to look at my new earring. "I don't remember you having this before."

"She gave it to me last night, sir."

"I'm sure you deserved it." He smiled, then looked around the table. "Did you see that Helen's boy has a new piercing?"

"Congratulations!" Robert beamed. The girls added their compliments. I had a hard time trying not to look too proud but was happy Lawrence had noticed. We chatted a few minutes as a waitress delivered their drinks.

"There'll be a small after-hours party following the performance," I said. "Helen would be more than honored if you'd stay."

"Well," Master Lawrence said as he looked around the table, "we have to be up early tomorrow, but I think we can stay for a little while."

Robert and the girls nodded happily.

"She'll be so pleased. I have to go see if she needs anything."

"Take good care of her." With that, I was dismissed.

For the final performance, I was so nervous I paced across the back of the room, listening but not listening, hearing only the music and listening for mistakes. My stomach pounded as if I was an expectant father, like I'd spawned this baby. Would this baby be golden?

I watched the faces, the smiles and laughter. I worried about one thing, and then I worried about something else. I was going to develop an ulcer.

As the music wound to the climax, everyone was on their feet, yelling and screaming and applauding with joy. Even after everyone left the stage. Helen walked out once to wave and thank everyone. The applause didn't die down until the manager turned up the lights and the waiters started handing out the bills.

I raced backstage to share the joy of the crowd with Helen.

❖

I was about to reach over the bar for my rum and ginger when a long, graceful arm took my drink from the bartender and held it out to me.

"I hear you do transcriptions."

I slowly turned, my eyes glued to the hand holding my

drink, my heart beating a quick gallop. I hoped my hand wasn't shaking so badly that I'd splash the syrupy blend all over the place. As I looked up into her clear, beautiful face, I was captured by dark eyes that seemed to bore through me.

"Well, My Little Butch?" She smiled. "Déjà vu?"

I nodded.

"It seems like it was such a long time ago, doesn't it?"

I had to nod again.

"And this is how it all started."

"Yes, ma'am," I said, taking a sip of the drink.

"Are you happy with the results?"

"Of course. The opera was spectacular!"

Helen laughed. "I wasn't referring to the music, Little Butch. I'm asking about our relationship."

I dropped my eyes to the floor. "Yes, ma'am. Very happy."

She stared. "Then I have another project for you."

"Another opera?"

"If you wish."

I looked up at her, not sure what she was getting to.

"You have two months till I get back. Two months to create, write, and record an hour and a half of music."

I wasn't sure what to say. "An hour and a half? Why?"

"Because I told you to." She flashed her most knowing grin. I guess the look on my face told more than I suspected. Helen burst out laughing. "Scared?"

"Yes!"

"Of what?" I heard from behind me.

Master Lawrence stood there. I looked between them. Helen stared, not making a move to explain to. "Mistress has given me an assignment, sir. She wants me to write some music." I realized I was mumbling.

Lawrence studied me, then turned to Helen and nodded. "Are you creating a monster, Helen?"

"I hope so."

Lawrence looked me up and down. "I'll be interested to see what'll come out of it. But now we must be going." He gave Helen a warm hug and motioned to Robert and the girls. They stepped forward to thank Helen for a wonderful evening, then made their way toward the door. Lawrence patted my shoulder, then leaned to my ear. "Be a good boy and make your mistress proud." With that, they were gone.

I looked up. Helen was smiling at me. "An hour and a half, huh?" I mused.

"I know you can do it…and Roz knows you can do it, so sharpen your pencils and get ready to start. I'll be expecting big things when I get back." She winked, turned, and left me standing there.

I took a very big gulp of my drink. Helen moved to the other side of the room. She whispered something to Roz, who turned to look at me. With a nod, Roz raised her glass in a toast. I returned the salute, then looked down into my drink, a wide, wide grin forming on my face, so wide it hurt my cheeks.

Chapter Twenty-two

The days seemed to drag with Helen away. She'd never been gone so long. When Will called up about the mail, I'd race to the lobby for a letter or postcard, always short and sweet, but enough to keep me from going crazy and let me know she was thinking about me. Every time I found something out of place in the apartment, it made me miss her more.

I kept busy. I worked hard to get new music down and went to the recording studio every week as Helen had arranged. I went to the bars a few times in the evenings, but I was bored. I even accepted an invitation from Carl and Robert to go to a movie, but I refused their offer to take me to a party. I missed Helen too much to even think about that. So I sat at home and worked.

Page after page, tape after tape. I became possessed. I was writing music *for* Helen. Not copying her music but writing music to her, selecting lyrics that spoke about my dedication to her and my love. I chose titles that echoed her. I worked frantically.

I took a weekend to visit my folks in Massachusetts, but I found myself in turmoil there, pacing around the house, not eating food that had been my favorite. My mom asked if anything was wrong, but I only told her I was worried about the music I was writing. She hugged me and assured me she thought it would turn out wonderful, like it always had. On Sunday night, I raced back to New York to recheck the music, check the mail, and wait for Helen to come home.

I transcribed a few pieces of music for one of Helen's friends...and I waited. I had an hour and a half of music ready for Helen's inspection as the day of her return loomed. I swept and cleaned the apartment, polishing everything to a bright shine, cleaning all the toys in the dungeon. I marked the calendar each day, counting down...five, four, three...

Then the phone rang.

The sound of her voice sent shivers through me.

"Mistress," I cried. "I've missed you so very much. I can't wait to see you!"

She chuckled. "Well, you'll have to, Little Butch. I've been delayed. I won't be home until Saturday."

"I thought you were coming home on Thursday."

"I was, Little Butch, but I've got some business to finish in Chicago. I won't be here long."

"Do you want me to meet your plane?"

"No, I'll get home faster if I catch a cab. I should be home around late afternoon."

"I'll be waiting for you."

"Good. It's been a long trip. See you then." And with that, the line went dead.

Damn! Four more days. What was I gonna do with myself?

It was 4:45 when the phone rang again. It was Will. "She's on her way up!"

I ran for the door and waited at the elevator as it opened. "Mistress!" I sank to my knees after making sure she was alone.

"Little Butch! You are a sight for tired eyes. Help me get these suitcases inside. It feels so good to be home." She walked past me as I pushed her three bags off the elevator.

She picked up the smallest one and walked down the hall into the apartment. By the time I'd lugged the other two inside, she had kicked off her shoes. "Look at this place," she said as I closed the door. "It's a mess. Look at all these flowers all over the place." She turned around and glared. Slowly, it turned into a broad smile for the dozens of roses, carnations, tulips, and other flowers I'd arranged around the apartment.

"Welcome home," I whispered.

She drew me into a warm embrace. "I just may have to punish you for all this extravagance."

"Oh yes, ma'am. Please. I beg your forgiveness." I smiled.

"Then wipe that Mickey Mouth grin off your face and start acting like a good boy. It's been a long flight. You can bring my bags upstairs while I freshen up. Did you think of feeding me? Or did you spend all of your money on flowers?"

"Dinner is ready whenever you want."

She ran her hand down my cheek. "I'd like to eat early. We have an appointment at 8:03."

I caught my breath as she turned and started up the stairs. My mistress was home.

❖

Time and energy seemed to have caught up with Helen on this tour. She looked older and laughed less. She seemed to be carrying the weight of the world on her shoulders. The slap of her hand and the sting of her whip didn't seem to have the force it had before.

I knew something was wrong. She'd been enthused about my music but seemed preoccupied. My music sat there, the tapes barely listened to. She'd been too quiet. Not like the quietness when she was writing music but a silence that seemed a brooding. Her reactions in the dungeon were strange. There were times when I thought she really would cut my head off and others when I sensed she didn't want to harm me at all. I asked if something was wrong, but she always said no and refused to talk about it.

One day, as I returned from an errand, she was waiting in the living room in her leather chair. "Is anything wrong?" I asked.

"Put your packages away. We need to talk."

My stomach turned. Had someone died? Had I done something wrong? Had she grown tired of me? I rushed to put the groceries in the kitchen and returned to the living room, sinking to the floor in front of her. As she reached for a cigarette, I jumped to hold the lighter. Then I waited as she sat back and inhaled. Her eyes dug into me. I couldn't guess what was wrong.

"I accepted a new position today," she said slowly. "I've taken a teaching job outside of Chicago."

My mind raced. "I've never been to Chicago."

"I'm going alone."

"How long will you be gone?"

She looked away. "Permanently. I've decided to give this apartment to Tina. I have to be in Chicago in six weeks."

My mind searched for the meaning of her words. "I don't understand. When will I join you?"

She took my face in her hands. "You won't, Little Butch. I will release you. Or find another mistress or master for you if you want. Roz is willing to pay your way to Los Angeles if you want to go to her. But I have to move to Chicago alone."

I felt my world crumbling around me. "Have I done

something to displease you? How can I make it up to you? Is my music that bad? I'll work on it. I can redo it."

"You've done nothing wrong, Little Butch; it's just time to move on." She took her hands from my face.

Tears and terror began to rise in me. "Whatever I've done, I'm sorry. I'll fix it. I'll be your good boy, I promise."

"I'm sorry. I'm moving to Chicago without you."

"But why? What have I done?"

"You haven't done anything wrong, boy. It's just time to change." She stood. "I'm getting too old to keep this pace. I'm tired of touring. I'm going to settle down, teach a few classes at the college, and write. I'll make sure your music reaches the right people."

"But who…who'll transcribe your music? Who'll… who'll…" I was floundering.

"Who'll warm my bed?"

"Mistress…"

She didn't respond.

"If…if there's someone there…someone else, I wouldn't be in the way. I could take care of a sister or brother. I wouldn't demand all your time. Just a little. Any crumb. I could still serve you. I could do a lot of other things. I—"

"Stop it! You need to pursue your own career. You're better than most. Everyone saw that when you played at the rehearsal. You should be touring on your own. You should have your own music published. There are lots of people in this town who will pay you very well to transcribe tapes—"

"I'm happy doing yours!"

"It's not enough. It's not enough for me, and it shouldn't be enough for you. I've heard your work. It's time you walked in your own light. You don't need to be in my shadow any longer."

I couldn't be hearing this. "I like being in your shadow!"

"Well, you shouldn't." Helen's face took on a stern look. "Get out of my shadow and start to make your own."

I jumped to my feet. "Then you never wanted me, did you? All you wanted was someone to copy your music. Someone to adore you and be at your beck and call. Someone to make your music look good."

She stared.

I was overcome with the realization of what I'd said. "I'm sorry. I didn't mean that. I really didn't mean that. I'm just so surprised. I don't know what I'm saying. Please. You said you were happy to come home. You were happy that I was waiting for you."

She took out the little silk sack she always wore on a chain around her neck. It held the key to my collar. She opened it and grasped the key, then grabbed my collar.

I shrank back. "No!"

"Please don't make this more difficult."

"I love you. I adore you. I'll do anything for you."

Her hand stayed on my collar. "Then let go. Don't make me rip this off you."

Tears fell from my eyes. "What have I done?"

"Nothing," she stated, her voice flat. "You've done nothing wrong. I just need to change things in my life. You need to change things in your life. Why must you turn this around?"

Everything was upside down. "I…I thought you loved me," I said, my breath coming in short gasps.

"I do in my own way. But this is something I have to do. If you really love me, you'll let go."

I pulled away, surprised she had such a weak grasp, and escaped into my room. What would I do? Where would I go? When would I wake up and find this was just a twisted nightmare?

I wanted to throw things. I wanted to hear breaking glass as I felt the breaking of my heart. I felt out of control, flailing ineffectively in the dark. My stomach churned. My head threatened to explode. And my heart pounded a loud beat that seemed to put the sounds of the city in jeopardy of being silenced.

My hand went to the collar. How could I breathe without this? I'd be naked…without an identity. I'd be without Helen.

I threw myself onto the bed, tears exploding from me.

❖

The next few days dragged by. There was no speech. We passed each other without recognition. There were times that I felt her reach out, but I was so hurt and angry that I didn't make it easy, and she withdrew again. Even when I heard her hard hack of a cough, I didn't ask if she was all right or if she needed something to drink.

People came to pack things in the apartment, and I gathered my belongings in a box and suitcase to ship back to Boston.

On the day I was to leave, I picked up the one thing I hadn't been able to pack and carried it into the living room. "What should I do with this?" I asked, holding the collar out.

She looked into my face for the first time in over a week. There was a long sigh. "What do you want to do with it?"

My mind went through a rapid whirl of conflicting thoughts. I wanted to ram it into her face or sink to my knees and have her place it around my neck again. "May I keep it? As a memory?"

Helen stood. "I hope that's not the only memory you'll keep."

What could I say that I hadn't anguished over in the past week? "It…it's the main one. I think I understand what you want. But it's very hard."

"I know, Mickey," she said, obviously having a hard time using my real name. "But it's best for both of us. Maybe there'll be a boy or girl in the future who you'll want to wear it." I started to shake my head, but she reached out and stopped me. "I know. This is the most difficult part. Please understand that I have to go alone. This is *my* journey. You'll have to find your own. The world is out there waiting for you. Find your own path. You're an excellent pianist, and you'll get even better. This town, this world, can be yours. It can be whatever you want to make it."

She picked up a couple sheets of paper. "This is a list of names that might help you, booking agents for some of the clubs in town, some of my friends who can use you to transcribe, and a few other people you should know in this industry. You're good, and you can make a name for yourself."

I looked at the papers and folded them carefully to put in my bag.

"There's also one name I highlighted on the last page. Give him a call and bring him your tapes. There are a couple pieces in there that could make you a lot of money if he can get the right people to record them. You have quite a talent."

I was almost too shocked to respond. "Thank you."

"I expect great things from you. Don't disappoint me." She pulled my face to hers and placed her lips on mine. Slowly, she drew me into her arms and hugged me close, enveloping me in a passionate and all-encompassing embrace. I accepted, giving back what I could but not forcing the ardor I really felt. Then she kissed me again, warmly, lovingly.

Finally, I drew back. There wasn't much more to say. It had been the kiss I'd wanted since the first night she handed me that drink. But the reason behind it, the meaning of that kiss, wasn't what I wanted it to be. It was a kiss of closure, not a promise of tomorrow.

I didn't know what was in store, where I was headed, or what I'd find there, but one thing was certain: Nothing would ever be "ordinary" again.

Chapter Twenty-Three

I'd been living in Brooklyn for several months with my new girl, a hot young woman with a body that craved abuse. I had an office job near Times Square and a life quite different from either Boston or the Upper West Side.

Every day, I thought of Helen. I read *Variety* religiously to try to keep up, to see if she was touring again, or if she had a new record released. I also kept track of Roz. I knew when she was in town and where she was performing, and I got up the nerve to go see her. She was greeting fans backstage after a performance. Her long, sequined gown was so completely different from what I was used to. At that moment, she was still Diva Rosalyn, the Queen of Jazz.

"Good heavens! A sight for sore eyes." She drew me into an embrace.

"Excellent performance, sir," I whispered.

"Do you live in New York now?"

"Brooklyn."

"Stick around for a few minutes. After I change, we can go out for a drink."

I nodded, then stepped back to get out of the way of other fans. She changed into black leather pantsuit, looking the same as I remembered. A young black woman stood just behind her.

"Mickey used to be Mistress Helen's boy," she told her new girl, Tasha. Tasha smiled but didn't say anything. "So where are you now? What are you doing these days? Are you performing anywhere?" Roz asked as she led us out into the alley behind the theater.

"I'm afraid not. I guess I'm still walking in her shadow."

"It's a big shadow, isn't it?"

"Yes, sir."

Roz stopped and looked at me. "Are you collared now? No. Then you don't need to call me sir. Unless you're collared, we're equals."

"I had a hard enough time remembering to call you Miss Maxwell." I laughed. "And I'm not under the delusion to think that I'm your equal."

"Don't be silly. Sure you are, unless you want to come to California."

I chuckled and looked at my shoes. "I'm not sure that would be prudent. But I'm honored by the invitation."

We entered a small bar around the corner from the theater. Once we'd settled at a table and ordered drinks, I got the boldness to ask, "Do you hear from her?"

"Every now and then." She took a deep breath. "No one has replaced you, you know."

I looked at my glass.

"I fear she's turning into a nun," Roz continued.

I smiled.

"You still love her, don't you?"

I nodded. "I always will."

"So will I."

We talked for a while, but the friendly banter of the Upper West Side was gone. It was hard finding something to talk about that didn't lead back to Helen. As we left, she handed me her card.

"If you ever need anything, give a call," she said.

"Thank you, sir, I mean, Ms. Maxwell. I will," I said, knowing I wouldn't.

She hugged me, and I watched as she and Tasha returned to their hotel. I knew I'd never see her again. It was just too painful for both of us.

❖

I hadn't heard from Helen in almost a year, but I'd read in the trade papers that she'd been admitted to a hospital in Chicago, so I sent a card. I was unprepared for the phone call that night.

"Hello, Little Butch," a familiar voice said.

"Mistress," I shouted, feeling the time fade away. I zoned into my bottom space. "It's good to hear your voice. How are you feeling?"

She laughed. It was the same but different. Weaker? Hoarser? "They've got me hooked up to so many tubes here, you wouldn't recognize me. I just wanted to know how you were doing."

"I'm doing fine. Just fine." I couldn't tell her how hearing her voice was tearing me apart with a longing for her again.

"Are you bottoming to anyone I know?"

I laughed. "No, I'm topping. I've got my own girl now." How could I explain that I could never imagine submitting to anyone except her, never able to adore anyone the way I'd adored her. Or could I tell her how I'd gone from person to person, acting out a death wish, lowering myself into one scene after another with no regard for my own safety? Searching for the one top whose touch would mean as much as hers. "You taught me well, Mistress."

"Good for you, Little Butch. Give her one from me."

We both laughed. Warmth ran through me, a rush of the love for her. The old love, the way it had been.

"Are you playing piano anywhere?"

"Just some backup right now," I said. "I've got two groups looking at my songs, though." How could I tell her that all I played now was classical music, accompanying students at the local college or opera singers on tour? How could I admit that my career as a jazz pianist was a flop, that I was growing tired of being compared to her, reviewed as being a weak carbon copy of the great Helen Robins. "I'm thinking of going back and finishing my doctorate."

"Really?"

"I've got a great topic for a thesis: 'The Music of Helen Robins.'"

"Well, you sure know more about it than anyone. I'll send you copies of the manuscripts and tapes, but you gotta promise me something."

"Of course, Mistress, anything you ask."

"Don't include any inside information on the *life* of Helen Robins."

I laughed. "How could I? Then I'd have to admit how much I crawled."

We laughed and talked for a few more minutes, but her voice grew weaker. Finally, she broke into a fit of coughing.

"Mickey?" Someone else had taken the phone. "It's Tina." Her voice softened. I could tell she didn't want Helen to hear, that there were other people in the room. "She can't continue. This has worn her out."

"Oh, Tina. How is she, really? How long will she be in the hospital? Can I come visit when she's home?"

There was a short silence. "She won't be going home, Mickey. She could go any time."

I stood there in my Brooklyn bedroom, shaking.

"Mickey? Are you all right? Are you still there?"

"I...didn't know."

"The cancer had gone all through her. They couldn't catch it in time."

"It was those damned cigarettes, wasn't it? I should have thrown them all away."

"You couldn't have stopped her. Don't blame yourself. I've been after her for years."

"Oh, Tina, I'm so sorry. Can I come now? I could catch a flight tonight."

"Mickey, she doesn't want anyone to see her. She even sent Roz home. And she wouldn't let me bring Jackie."

Tears ran down my face.

"I'm sure she knew she wasn't well when she was with you. I think that's why she canceled her European tour and moved away from New York. She didn't want anyone she knew to see her fail," Tina continued. "She never even told me she wasn't feeling well until I came to visit last fall. I was concerned that she'd lost so much weight. It took all my nagging to get her to tell me what the doctors said."

"Tina..." What could I say? "Would you tell her...I still love her?"

"She knows that, Mickey." Tina's voice was low and solemn. "She knows that. That's why she had to call you."

"Tell her..." I knew it was true. "I'll only wear *her* collar for the rest of my life."

There was a beat of silence. "I'll do that. It'll please her."

"Thank you."

"I'll write you when this is over," Tina said, resignation in her voice. "She's asked to be cremated. I'll let you know what I do with the ashes."

I couldn't talk. My throat felt blocked.

"Take care of yourself, Mickey." The line went dead.

I looked at the phone, not wanting to put it back in its cradle, wishing I could keep the connection open. I sank onto the bed and let the tears fall. Not the sobbing I'd cried so many times in Helen's dungeon, but tears that started in my heart and spilled, unchecked, out of my eyes. I couldn't comprehend it. How could Helen be dying? How could life continue without her? How could *I* continue without her? Even though I hadn't seen her in two years, everything I did was to win her approval, to make her proud of me. That was my goal in life, to hear her say, just one more time, "You please me, boy."

I sobbed myself to sleep.

About the Author

Nanisi Barrett D'Arnuk had a successful music career as a pianist and conductor and performed and traveled around the world several times. She has lived in the Northeast, the Pacific Northwest, and the South Central US. Although she lived in Texas for ten years, she had to go to Brazil to experience a cattle drive.

When MS curtailed traveling and performing, she turned to her writing. She has written mysteries, romances, and erotica. She now lives on thirty acres of wooded land in South Central Oklahoma with her partner, their son, two labs, and a puggle.

Books Available From Bold Strokes Books

Flight to the Horizon by Julie Tizard. Airline captain Kerri Sullivan and flight attendant Janine Case struggle to survive an emergency water landing and overcome dark secrets to give love a chance to fly. (978-1-63555-331-4)

In Helen's Hands by Nanisi Barrett D'Arnuk. As her mistress, Helen pushes Mickey to her sensual limits, delivering the pleasure only a BDSM lifestyle can provide her. (978-1-63555-639-1)

Jamis Bachman, Ghost Hunter by Jen Jensen. In Sage Creek, Utah, a poltergeist stirs to life and past secrets emerge.(978-1-63555-605-6)

Moon Shadow by Suzie Clarke. Add betrayal, season with survival, then serve revenge smokin' hot with a sharp knife. (978-1-63555-584-4)

Spellbound by Jean Copeland and Jackie D. When the supernatural worlds of good and evil face off, love might be what saves them all. (978-1-63555-564-6)

Temptation by Kris Bryant. Can experienced nanny Cassie Miller deny her growing attraction and keep her relationship with her boss professional? Or will they sidestep propriety and give in to temptation? (978-1-63555-508-0)

The Inheritance by Ali Vali. Family ties bring Tucker Delacroix and Willow Vernon together, but they could also tear them, and any chance they have at love, apart. (978-1-63555-303-1)

Thief of the Heart by MJ Williamz. Kit Hanson makes a living seducing rich women in casinos and relieving them of the expensive jewelry most won't even miss. But her streak ends when she meets beautiful FBI agent Savannah Brown. (978-1-63555-572-1)

Face Off by PJ Trebelhorn. Hockey player Savannah Wells rarely spends more than a night with any one woman, but when photographer Madison Scott buys the house next door, she's forced to rethink what she expects out of life. (978-1-63555-480-9)

Hot Ice by Aurora Rey, Elle Spencer, and Erin Zak. Can falling in love melt the hearts of the iciest ice queens? Join Aurora Rey, Elle Spencer, and Erin Zak to find out! A contemporary romance novella collection. (978-1-63555-513-4)

Line of Duty by VK Powell. Dr. Dylan Carlyle's professional and personal life is turned upside down when a tragic event at Fairview Station pits her against ambitious, handsome police officer Finley Masters. ((978-1-63555-486-1)

London Undone by Nan Higgins. London Craft reinvents her life after reading a childhood letter to her future self and, in doing so, finds the love she truly wants. (978-1-63555-562-2)

Lunar Eclipse by Gun Brooke. Moon De Cruz lives alone on an uninhabited planet after being shipwrecked in space. Her life changes forever when Captain Beaux Lestarion's arrival threatens the planet and Moon's freedom. (978-1-63555-460-1)

One Small Step by MA Binfield. In this contemporary romance, Iris and Cam discover the meaning of taking chances and following your heart, even if it means getting hurt. (978-1-63555-596-7)

Shadows of a Dream by Nicole Disney. Rainn has the talent to take her rock band all the way, but falling in love is a powerful distraction, and her new girlfriend's meth addiction might just take them both down. 978-1-63555-598-1)

Someone to Love by Jenny Frame. When Davina Trent is given an unexpected family, can she let nanny Wendy Darling teach her to open her heart to the children and to Wendy? (978-1-63555-468-7)

Uncharted by Robyn Nyx. As Rayne Marcellus and Chase Stinsen track the legendary Golden Trinity, they must learn to put their differences aside and depend on one another to survive. (978-1-63555-325-3)

Where We Are by Annie McDonald. A sensual account of two women who discover a way to walk on the same path together with the help of an Indigenous tale, a Canadian art movement, and the mysterious appearance of dimes. (978-1-63555-581-3)

A Moment in Time by Lisa Moreau. A longstanding family feud separates two women who unexpectedly fall in love at an antique clock shop in a small Louisiana town. (978-1-63555-419-9)

Aspen in Moonlight by Kelly Wacker. When art historian Melissa Warren meets Sula Johansen, director of a local bear conservancy, she discovers that love can come in unexpected and unusual forms. (978-1-63555-470-0)

Back to September by Melissa Brayden. Small bookshop owner Hannah Shepard and famous romance novelist Parker Bristow maneuver the landscape of their two very different worlds to find out if love can win out in the end. (978-1-63555-576-9)

Changing Course by Brey Willows. When the woman of her dreams falls from the sky, intergalactic space captain Jessa Arbelle had better be ready to catch her. (978-1-63555-335-2)

Cost of Honor by Radclyffe. First Daughter Blair Powell and Homeland Security Director Cameron Roberts face adversity when their enemies stop at nothing to prevent President Andrew Powell's reelection. Book 11 in the Honor series. (978-1-63555-582-0)

Fearless by Tina Michele. Determined to overcome her debilitating fear through exposure therapy, Laura Carter all but fails before she's even begun until dolphin trainer Jillian Marshall dedicates herself to helping Laura defeat the nightmares of her past. (978-1-63555-495-3)

Not Dead Enough by J.M. Redmann. In the tenth book of the Micky Knight mystery series, a woman who may or may not be dead drags Micky into a messy con game. (978-1-63555-543-1)

Not Since You by Fiona Riley. When Charlotte boards her honeymoon cruise single and comes face-to-face with Lexi, the high school love she left behind, she questions every decision she has ever made. (978-1-63555-474-8)

Tennessee Whiskey by Donna K. Ford. After losing her job, Dane Foster starts spiraling out of control. She wants to put her life on pause and ask for a redo, a chance for something that matters. Emma Reynolds is that chance. (978-1-63555-556-1)

IN HELEN'S HANDS

Visit us at www.boldstrokesbooks.com